KILLER

ON THE RUN

KILLER
ON THE RUN

M A COMLEY

2018

New York Times and USA Today bestselling author M A Comley
Published by Jeamel Publishing limited
Copyright © 2018 M A Comley
Digital Edition, License Notes

This is a work of fiction. Names, characters, places and incidents are a product of the author's imagination or are used fictitiously, and any resemblance to actual persons living or dead, business establishments, events or locales is entirely coincidental.

ISBN-13: 978-1983647857

ISBN-10: 1983647853

OTHER BOOKS BY M A COMLEY

Blind Justice (Novella)
Cruel Justice (Book #1)
Mortal Justice (Novella)
Impeding Justice (Book #2)
Final Justice (Book #3)
Foul Justice (Book #4)
Guaranteed Justice (Book #5)
Ultimate Justice (Book #6)
Virtual Justice (Book #7)
Hostile Justice (Book #8)
Tortured Justice (Book #9)
Rough Justice (Book #10)
Dubious Justice (Book #11)
Calculated Justice (Book #12)
Twisted Justice (Book #13)
Justice at Christmas (Short Story)
Prime Justice (Book #14)
Heroic Justice (Book #15)
Shameful Justice (Book #16 coming May 2018)
Unfair Justice (a 10,000 word short story)
Irrational Justice (a 10,000 word short story)
Clever Deception (co-written by Linda S Prather)
Tragic Deception (co-written by Linda S Prather)
Sinful Deception (co-written by Linda S Prather)
Forever Watching You (DI Miranda Carr thriller)
Wrong Place (DI Sally Parker thriller #1)
No Hiding Place (DI Sally Parker thriller #2)
Cold Case (DI Sally Parker #3)

Deadly Encounter (DI Sally Parker thriller series #4)
Web of Deceit (DI Sally Parker Novella with Tara Lyons)
The Missing Children (DI Kayli Bright #1)
Killer On The Run (DI Kayli Bright #2)
Hidden Agenda (DI Kayli Bright #3)
The Caller (co-written with Tara Lyons)
Evil In Disguise – a novel based on True events
Deadly Act (Hero series novella)
Torn Apart (Hero series #1)
End Result (Hero series #2)
In Plain Sight (Hero Series #3)
Double Jeopardy (Hero Series #4)
Sole Intention (Intention series #1)
Grave Intention (Intention series #2)
Devious Intention (Intention #3)
Merry Widow (A Lorne Simpkins short story)
It's A Dog's Life (A Lorne Simpkins short story)
A Time To Heal (A Sweet Romance)
A Time For Change (A Sweet Romance)
High Spirits
The Temptation series (Romantic Suspense/New Adult Novellas)
Past Temptation (available now)
Lost Temptation (available now)

KEEP IN TOUCH WITH THE AUTHOR:

Twitter
https://twitter.com/Melcom1

Blog
http://melcomley.blogspot.com

Facebook
http://smarturl.it/sps7jh

Newsletter
http://smarturl.it/8jtcvv

BookBub
www.bookbub.com/authors/m-a-comley

ACKNOWLEDGMENTS

Thank you as always to my rock, Jean, who keeps me supplied with endless cups of coffee while I punish my keyboard. I'd be lost without you in my life.

Special thanks as always go to my talented editor, Stefanie Spangler Buswell and to Karri Klawiter for her superb cover design expertise.

My heartfelt thanks go to my wonderful proofreader, Joseph, for spotting all the lingering nits.

Thank you to Kayli and Donna from my ARC group for allowing me to use your names in this novel.

And finally, to all the wonderful Bloggers and Facebook groups for their never-ending support of my work.

PROLOGUE

Carmen raised her glass of orange juice and chinked it against her friends'. Dawn and Sonia beamed at her over the rims of their glasses. They had been friends since school, welcoming and celebrating each other's triumphs along the way, and that night, they were there to celebrate Carmen's promotion at work.

"To the new supervisor to the mortgage advisor," Dawn said, slurring her words more than a little, which wasn't surprising after the number of drinks she'd thrown down her neck over the past few hours.

"Hear, hear! Congratulations, Carmen," Sonia said, then she leaned over to whisper, "You'll soon be stepping up into Warren's shoes."

Carmen laughed. "I doubt that will happen. Hey, I need to drink this and be on my way. Some of us have important work to do in the morning."

"Ooo ... get you! We have important roles in life too, you know. I doubt you would have achieved your promotion without our valuable input. Your hair was a damn mess last week before you visited the salon, and don't even get me started on your *nails*. Frankly, I've seen better nails on a Labrador."

Carmen's eyes widened. "Hey, great analogy—*not*. I know I couldn't have done this without you girls always being by my side. We've supported each other, since—what? We were five or six? I'd be lost without you."

Dawn elbowed Sonia. "Oh gosh, here she goes, getting all emosh on us."

Carmen sipped her drink and searched for a hankie in her handbag. She dabbed at her eyes, trying to keep her mascara intact. "Shut up! Stop taking the piss. Isn't a girl allowed to get emotional now and again with her best mates? You guys are like family to me."

Sonia put down her glass and mimed playing a violin with her arms. "Aww ... here she goes."

Carmen laughed, gulped down the rest of her drink, and stood up. "I have to go. Are you sure you two don't want a lift home?"

"Nope. The night is still young for us yet. We're not wimps ... like you." Dawn sniggered mischievously.

"Charming! If I didn't have an important meeting to attend in the morning with my, er ... new boss, I'd stay on and party with you. Anyway, I'm going to love you and leave you. Do you want to meet up on Saturday? I'd like to try out that new Indian restaurant that's just opened up on the edge of town, if you're up for it? Apparently, it's receiving great reviews online."

"Phooey! You don't want to take notice of bloody reviews. This early on, half of them will have been written by the owner's friends anyway," Sonia slurred.

"Is that a yes or a no?"

"It's a yes from me," Dawn said with a firm nod.

"Oh, go on then. I could do with eating a curry for a good clear-out," Sonia said, shocking the other two girls.

"On that note, I think it's time I was leaving. Thank you for a fabulous evening as always and for helping me to celebrate my success. You girls rock." Carmen pecked her two friends on the cheek and walked towards the pub's exit, where her car was parked at the rear.

The night was inky black, and the sky was littered with tiny stars to guide her way. Before she could open her car door, she heard sudden footsteps behind her, causing her heart rate to escalate. She gulped and closed her eyes, fearing that someone was about to assault her. Then she remembered a self-defence lesson the building society had insisted she attend. The instructor had instilled in them how much damage a car key could do if it was jabbed in the right orifice. Swiftly, she manoeuvred her key in her right hand and turned, raising her hand, ready to use the key. She blew out a relieved sigh when she saw Dawn standing behind her. "Jesus, babe, you almost had my key in your eye. Why didn't you call out or speak to me?"

"Sorry. It took all my energy and strength to remain upright after all the wine I've drunk this evening."

Carmen hugged her with relief. "Idiot. Did you forget to tell me something?"

Dawn leaned against Carmen's car with a thud, misjudging how close she was to the vehicle. Carmen stifled a giggle. Dawn despised it when people laughed at her drunken antics. "I didn't want to ask in front of Sonia. What did Lincoln say?"

Carmen's gaze drifted down to her feet, and she kicked out at a nearby stone. "Umm ... I haven't told him my other secret yet."

"What? Why? It's been weeks since you found out."

"I know. I'm building up to it, hon. One thing at a time. Let him get used to my promotion first, then I'll tackle the other subject."

Dawn pushed away from the car and flung her arms around Carmen's neck. "It's your call. I'll be here to support you, no matter what happens. Love you now and for always."

"Love you now and for always, too," Carmen repeated the little ditty they had frequently said to each other for the past ten years or so. "Go, you better get back to Sonia now. She'll be wondering what's going on otherwise."

"Give me a ring tomorrow," Dawn shouted over her shoulder as she weaved her way back to the pub through the parked cars. "Shit! That was my frigging toe."

Carmen laughed and slipped behind the steering wheel of her car. She started the engine and pulled out of the car park and onto the B-road that ran past the pub, which was on the outskirts of town. She turned up the volume on the car stereo, filling the inside of the car with One Direction. Her fingers tapped along to the music on the steering wheel as she drove. She switched on the heating as a sudden chill washed over her. *That'll teach me to go out wearing a flimsy dress, thinking it's still summer.* The autumn equinox had just passed, which meant the nights were definitely becoming colder with winter just around the corner.

She travelled along the bypass that led to her house, a tiny two-bed she'd bought when she was only twenty-three. She had saved hard to find the deposit, but property in the Bristol area had rapidly increased in value since she'd taken the plunge to put down roots. Dawn and Sonia had slated her at the time, called her daft for having mortgage repayments around her neck at such a young age. That had all changed recently, though. They had both intimated that they were regretting their decision not to get on the property ladder sooner, like she had. They shared a two-bed flat in an unsightly tower block in the city. It had been erected back in the sixties and should have been condemned years ago.

Something in the rear-view mirror caught her eye. Her gaze flicked between the road ahead and her mirror. *Maybe it was a bright star? There's nothing there now.* She travelled another half a mile or so before she saw the same bright light again. This time it didn't disappear but remained behind her.

Idiot! It's a damn motorbike. Relieved that it wasn't some kind of UFO and that she wasn't about to be abducted by aliens, she relaxed, and her fingers began tapping to the beat of the music once more. Every now and again, her gaze drifted to her mirror to find the light still behind her, keeping a safe distance.

Her favourite tune filled the car, and she upped the volume a touch. Sitting back, she saw the light had disappeared again. *How strange. We haven't passed any turn-offs yet. Maybe they changed their mind and turned around to head back after taking the wrong road.*

With the bike no longer distracting her, she focussed on the meeting ahead of her in the morning. For days, she'd been making notes for the presentation she was expected to give. The words started to run through her mind, blocking out the music. Then something caught her eye in the rear-view mirror again. The damn motorbike was back ... and getting closer. *Maybe it'll overtake me now. I wonder where it went before. Either way, I hope it goes past me soon.*

As her turning was coming up soon, Carmen kept one eye on the road and the other on the motorbike. The bright headlight was coming closer and closer, lighting up the interior of her car. *All right, buster, get on with it. Go past me. It's not as if you haven't got the room.*

Suddenly, the driver began to swerve, drift from one side of the lane to the other. "What the hell are you doing?" she shouted, her eyes drawn to the driver's shenanigans rather than the road ahead.

The bike eased off the accelerator and dropped back a few feet. She blew out a relieved sigh, but that relief didn't last long. The bike came hurtling towards her again. Distracted, Carmen veered off course and slammed into the barrier. A scream lodged itself in her throat as the car descended the steep incline. Carmen swallowed the bile filling her throat, and finally the scream erupted. "Please, God, help me!"

The car struck something hard, and it began to roll the rest of the way down the embankment. Thoughts of her dearly departed mother and father entered her confused mind, and she wondered if they would be there to greet her when she finally came to rest. "I don't want to die. I have too much to live for. Please, someone help me," she cried out, her voice juddering.

The car gained momentum, tumbling down the steep slope, until it finally came to an abrupt halt, resting on its roof. Her seat belt cutting into her shoulder, Carmen was drifting into unconsciousness, many questions running through her mind. The one that stood out the most was whether someone would find her. And when.

CHAPTER ONE

Kayli Bright tapped the button on the alarm to silence it. She reached out for her fiancé, but her hand landed on a cold spot in the bed. Her eyes filled with tears. She missed Mark. Her life just wasn't the same without him in it.

Not wanting to be reminded of what had gone on the past few weeks, she leapt out of bed and ran into the bathroom. While the shower water heated up, she studied her face in the mirror. Her cheeks had become gaunt. Without realising it, she had lost a lot of weight in the last few weeks. She pulled the scales into the centre of the room and jumped on. Through half-closed eyes, she glanced down at the electronic reading and gasped. "Shit! I've lost half a stone—seven whole pounds. What the fuck? You can't keep doing that, Kayli. You need to get your act together and quickly."

The shower was lukewarm, just what the doctor ordered to invigorate oneself in the morning, according to an article she'd read recently in one of her magazines. She washed herself quickly, then after drying herself she left the bathroom and shuddered. "I feel anything but invigorated. I'm bloody freezing. Maybe I would be better off ignoring the crappy advice I read in the magazines." She blow-dried her waist-length black hair and applied the lightest of makeup before she riffled through her wardrobe for a miracle outfit that would disguise how much weight she'd lost.

After deciding on a grey pinstriped suit, she chose one of her jumpers and tried it on. Then she struggled into her jacket, but it proved to be impossible to straighten her arms. Frustrated, she ripped off her jumper and selected a blouse she could wear loosely around her middle. The outfit successfully gave the impression that she had put on ten pounds ... or was that her imagination playing tricks on her?

Neglecting to stop by the kitchen for breakfast, Kayli left the house, jumped into her car, and set off to the station. Kayli reflected how lucky she was to be on her way to a job she enjoyed. She loved being a detective inspector in the Murder Investigation Team. She was lucky to be blessed with a super-efficient team, whom she got on really well with, and a commendable DCI, even if Sandra Davis could be a little strict at times. Kayli's working life kept her occupied during the day and sometimes well into the evening. However, going home to an empty house was less than appealing most days.

She pulled into her allocated place just as her partner, Dave Chaplin, entered the car park. "Morning, Dave," she called as they both got out of their cars. "How are Suranne and Luke?"

"Morning, boss. Fair to middling, I guess. Luke is still teething, so we're not getting much sleep at the moment. Suranne seems to think he'll settle down soon enough. She gets up to deal with him during the night, so no big deal for me."

"Ever thought of giving Suranne a break during the night now and again, matey?"

"Yeah, I've thought about it, but the thought never lasts long before sleep descends upon me."

"Typical. Men are from Mars, after all," Kayli grumbled, turning her back on him and heading towards the main entrance of the station.

"No need for you to get your knickers in a twist about my sleep patterns, boss."

"It's not *that* I'm getting my knickers in a twist about, idiot. It's the fact that I'm sure Suranne would love a full eight hours now and then too. Except someone is too selfish to put his own needs aside for a while to give her a break. Hey, but what do I know about raising kids? Thankfully nothing, because I realise that I'm too selfish to have them. I have no plans of ever becoming pregnant."

"What do you expect me to say to that?"

"Nothing. I was merely stating facts."

"I'll have you know I do my share around the house."

They walked up the concrete stairs to the second floor, where the incident room was located.

"I'm not saying you don't. It must be really time-consuming putting the rubbish out for the binmen every Monday before you come in to work."

"Whoa! Who the fuck has rattled your cage this morning?"

Kayli bit down on her lip and turned to face him. "Ugh, sorry, matey, you didn't deserve that low blow. Just ignore me. Blame it on the cool shower I had this morning."

"Apology accepted. Want me to drop by and take a look at your boiler if it's giving you hassle?"

"Nothing wrong with the boiler. I read a stupid article that I should have slung in the bin instead. I'll be fine once I've downed a couple of coffees."

"Missed out on breakfast again, did you?"

"I was running late. Didn't have time to boil the kettle or drop some toast in the machine."

"Yeah, not for the first time lately. Do you realise how thin you've got, to the point of being scrawny?"

Kayli stopped mid-stride and looked at him, her mouth gaping open. "For one thing, you shouldn't be checking out my arse, and for another, it's none of your concern. Don't you know a lady takes offence when her weight is mentioned by a man?"

He raised his hands in front of him, his cheeks changing in colour to reflect his embarrassment. "Okay, I'll keep my nose out. I needed to say something, boss. You're wasting away. You need to get the doc to check you over, is all I'm saying."

"It's not that bad. I wanted to lose a few pounds anyway."

He placed his hand up to his mouth, and coughing at the same time he said, "Bullshit!"

Kayli swiped his arm. "Don't wind me up, Dave, not first thing in the morning and before I've dished out the jobs for the day. You're standing on dodgy ground right now, hon."

As soon as they entered the incident room, Kayli headed for the vending machine. "Anybody else want one?" she called out to the rest of the team already sitting at their desks.

DC Donna Travis was the first to answer. "I've already had one, but I could do with another, boss, if you're offering."

"I never say no. You know me, boss," DC Graeme Chance replied.

"Great, three cups coming up."

"Hey, aren't you forgetting someone?" Dave said, pouting like a kid on the verge of tears.

"After the crap you've just given me outside, you think I should treat you nicely?"

Donna and Graeme looked his way, expecting him to enlighten them.

Dave shrugged. "All I said was that she has a skinny arse. Am I wrong, guys?"

Kayli cleared her throat to gain everyone's attention. "I'd consider your answers carefully if I were you, guys. I haven't inserted the coins yet."

Graeme raised his hands and shook his head. "I ain't going there. I know what Lindy is like when I bring up the subject of her losing weight. Dave, there are some topics men should avoid commenting on like the plague."

Kayli nodded. "See, what did I tell you? I knew you were an intelligent man, Graeme. Unlike some I could mention."

"Jeez, looks like I'm in for a hell of a ride today, judging by your mood, boss. Will an apology suffice?" Dave fluttered his eyelashes.

Kayli hitched up her shoulder. "Only if it's meant sincerely."

"Are you touchy about your weight too, Donna?"

Donna's eyes widened, and she nodded slowly. "Yep, you really don't want to go there, Dave, not if you know what's good for you."

"I genuinely had no idea. I regret my slip of the tongue in that case, boss. I'm also begging you for your forgiveness." He dropped to his knees.

The team burst into laughter; even Kayli's stern face broke into a smile. She distributed the cups of coffee and helped Dave to stand up. "You're forgiven—this time. Right, let's see what's happening, shall we?"

"Boss, something I've just picked up on the screen might be of interest."

Kayli strode across the room to stand beside Donna. "What's that?"

"I'm hearing about a car going off the road on the B4054. Looks like it happened during the night. The rescue teams are at the scene now, and early reports are indicating that it's suspicious."

"We should get over there, Dave."

"Why? If there are no fatalities, then it's nothing to do with MIT, or am I missing something?"

"The word *suspicious* highlights that it could be attempted murder to me. Maybe that's just me overthinking things at this point. We won't know until we see the scene for ourselves. Sup up," she ordered.

Both of them blew on their cups of coffee and downed half their drinks.

Dave placed his cup on his desk. "Too hot for me, boss. I haven't got an asbestos gob. Are you ready?"

Kayli winced as the scalding liquid scorched her throat. "Not really, but that's not going to stop me." She set her cup aside also.

They raced down the stairs and drove to the accident scene. One lane of the B4054 had been sectioned off by cones, and the emergency service vehicles were all at the scene. Even the air ambulance was in attendance.

Kayli and Dave flashed their IDs for the uniformed police officer, and he lifted the crime scene tape for them. They rushed down the steep embankment to the overturned vehicle. One look at the wreckage told Kayli to prepare herself for the worst.

"Hello, Kayli, nice to see you again. Terrible incident, not sure if the woman is going to make it or not," DS Greg Boulder said, shaking his head.

"We heard reports that the incident is being treated as suspicious, Greg. Can you tell me why?"

"Preliminary tests indicate that the woman hadn't been drinking, and by that I mean we couldn't detect any alcohol on her breath."

Kayli raised an eyebrow. "And that's it? What about if she swerved to avoid something in the road? A cat or dog or badger perhaps?"

Greg shrugged. "It's possible. There are several different scenarios being bandied about at present. We won't know for sure what exactly happened until the young lady wakes up. The accident specialist team should be here soon."

Kayli surveyed the car from a distance then moved forward to examine the rear of the vehicle.

Dave followed her. "What are you thinking or looking for?"

"Evidence of impact, something to suggest she was shunted from behind."

"That's going to be impossible to determine, given that the car rolled halfway down the slope."

"I still need to check, Dave. Why else would someone deliberately drive into a barrier?"

"I hear you, but maybe this is just a genuine accident. They do happen, you know."

"I'm not disputing that, but something about this looks odd, and I have no clue why. She was driving alone, not something I tend to do late at night."

"It doesn't mean to say that other females have an aversion to driving alone in the dark."

"I know. Bear with me while I just run through a few things out loud that are bugging me, all right?"

"Fire away. I'm all ears."

They moved closer to the vehicle. "We need to find out if she's local or just passing through. Saying that, I'm local and had no idea there was this kind of drop the other side of the barrier, and I use this road regularly."

"I'm inclined to agree with you there. I didn't have a clue, either. However, the barrier would suggest there's a pretty huge drop."

"Granted. Let's see if we can get closer without hindering the rescue attempt."

"There's one scenario you haven't mentioned: suicide."

"Hmm ... I could think of better places—and ways—for someone to attempt that type of thing."

Inching forward, Kayli winced when she saw the angle the young woman was lying at and the way the roof of the car had caved in and was pressing down on the side of her head. She overheard a couple of firemen assessing the situation. They would need the Jaws of Life to rescue her from the wreckage, once the attending doctor had given the young woman pain relief. From what Kayli could tell, the woman's life hung in the balance, and she was dipping in and out of unconsciousness. If it had been up to Kayli, she wouldn't have hesitated getting the machinery in there immediately, but she wasn't an expert on dangerous, life-threatening situations.

"Is she going to be all right, Doc?" she asked, peering over the young doctor's shoulder.

"Hard to say at this point. I suspect she has some internal bleeding, and who knows what other injuries she has sustained. That won't become clear until she's free of this damn vehicle ..." He paused to inject the woman's arm. "Right, the pain relief has been administered. Now can we get her out of this wreckage, quickly."

Kayli and Dave stood back to allow a member of the fire brigade access to the vehicle. The machinery started up, and the noise was deafening. Kayli moved around to the other side of the vehicle to keep a watchful eye on the victim's reaction. She was sad to see there wasn't any. That didn't bode well, but on the other hand, the doctor had given her pain relief that had likely made her oblivious to what was going on around her.

It took a fireman with the Jaws of Life ten minutes to cut through two different parts of the vehicle. After the fireman retreated, his colleagues peeled back the metal and were able to extract the victim from the carnage. She was placed on a stretcher and swiftly transported up the embankment to the waiting chopper. Kayli and Dave followed the doctor and the paramedics. "We'll join you at the hospital, Doctor. We'll need a word with her as soon as her condition permits."

"Very well. I have no idea when that is likely to be, due to the medication and her head injuries. I'd like to keep her sedated for as long as possible to assess her injuries further. She'll probably go down to X-Ray the minute she arrives, and we'll go from there."

"I understand. There's nothing we can do here anyway. Damn, I need her ID. Dave, can you run back and see if there's a handbag in the car or some form of identification in the glove compartment? Failing that, note down her registration, and we'll search for the information we need that way."

Dave nodded and ran back down the slope to the car. He rejoined her a few minutes later, out of breath and carrying the woman's small handbag, which revealed very little. "Hang on ... yes, here's her driving licence tucked away in her purse." He handed Kayli the tiny card.

"It's a start. Let's get a contact number and ring her next of kin."

"I'll arrange that with Donna now. Are you all right, boss?"

Kayli shook her head and glanced at him. "Fine. Why do you ask?"

"Just concerned, that's all."

"There's nothing for you to be concerned about, Dave. I'm simply trying to figure out how the incident occurred."

He smiled tautly and punched the number of the station into his phone. Kayli watched the medics complete the job of strapping the stretcher in the back of the chopper, then turned to observe the impact the woman's car had made with the barrier. She tried to recall if there had ever been any other accidents on this stretch of road before. The answer was no—not that she could remember, anyway. Usually, if a section of road was dangerous enough to cause several accidents, there would be remnants of bouquets of flowers at the site. Kayli saw none on either side of the road, which only raised her suspicions more.

"Here we go. Donna worked her magic and found the woman's phone number."

"Great. Strange ... so she *is* local. Then she should know this road inside out, right?"

"You'd think. But that's a hell of an assumption."

"I know. I'm just trying to think outside the box. Okay, I need to ring her home number, see if there is anyone at the house. If not, we'll have to ask Donna to dig a little deeper or drop by the woman's address to question her neighbours." She dialled the number.

A man's sleepy voice answered the phone on the fourth ring; it was ten o'clock in the morning. "Hello?"

"Hi, sorry to disturb you, sir. Do you know a Carmen Drinkwater?"

"Yes, of course I know her. She's my girlfriend. Who is this?"

"I'm DI Kayli Bright of the Avon and Somerset Constabulary. It is with regret that I have to inform you that your girlfriend was involved in a serious accident."

"My God! Is she okay? How serious? She's not ... dead, is she?"

"No, not dead. We're at the scene now. Carmen is being airlifted to Bristol Royal Infirmary. Maybe you can join us there? We're just going to head over there now."

"Of course. Shit! How serious is it? She's going to be okay, isn't she?"

"We're not sure yet, sir. We'll know more once the medical staff have assessed her thoroughly at the hospital."

"I'll be right there. I'll have to make arrangements for a member of my staff to open up for me. I run a bar in the city centre. After that I'll come straight to the hospital. Where shall I meet you?"

"At the Accident and Emergency Department. Sorry, I should have asked, what's your name, sir?"

"Lincoln James. I'll be with you in half an hour, Inspector."

"See you then, Mr. James." Kayli hung up.

"How did he sound?"

"Upset. I woke him up. He's a bar manager, hence him still being in bed, I suppose. He's going to join us at the hospital. Talking of which, we should get a move on ourselves," she said, shielding her eyes from the dirt as the chopper took off.

During the short trip to the hospital, Kayli's mind was still on how the woman's car had left the road. The impact must have been major if the barrier had failed to stop the vehicle. It was one of those mind-boggling, annoying scenarios that distracted her to the point she almost ran into a car at the traffic lights.

"Hey, are you sure you're up to driving? I can take over. In fact, I'd rather do that if our aim is to get to the hospital in one piece, boss."

"Sorry. My mind is firmly on the crash site. I promise you I'll behave from now on." She bared her teeth in an embarrassed smile.

"As long as that's all it is," Dave grumbled, turning his head sideways as he spoke.

"Let's hear it, partner. If there's something on your mind that I should be aware of, then spit it out."

He shrugged. "Nope. Nothing that I can think of. I'm sitting here, minding my own business, as usual."

"Smart arse. Give me a break, eh? Let's concentrate on the job in hand and not what you perceive is going on in my head regarding my personal life."

"Ah, at last. You're finally admitting that there's something going on at home then?"

"I said that we should concentrate on the job for now, Dave. When I feel like sharing, you'll be the first to know."

"I didn't think we had any secrets. Guess I was wrong about that. I still ain't comfortable with the amount of weight you've lost. Slate me all you like for caring, but that's the truth."

She placed a hand on his knee briefly before she pulled away from the lights. "I genuinely appreciate what you're saying, Dave. There's nothing wrong with my weight. I just don't have much appetite at the moment, that's all."

"Have you seen the doctor? We're on our way to the hospital. Maybe you should take a doc aside to get the low-down on what could be wrong with you, because something sure is."

"Crap, you never give up, do you? You're like a crocodile in a death roll. If you must know, I'm worried stupid about Mark. There. Don't ask me to enlighten you on the subject as I'm liable to break down, and I don't relish speaking to Carmen's boyfriend in that state, okay?"

Dave bashed his thigh with his fist. "As soon as we leave the hospital, we need to have a chat about this situation, boss. It's not healthy for you to be so pent up with worry just because your pig-headed boyfriend has taken up a role that is more dangerous than assembling sticks of dynamite on an assembly line."

Kayli laughed, earning a scowl from her partner. "I appreciate you caring so much about my welfare, hon. Back to concentrating on the job in hand for now, right?"

"You win. I'll keep my mouth shut, for the time being. You know you can talk to me at any time, right? I promise to listen and not judge. I shouldn't have said what I did about Mark. I know he'd been out of work for a while and took the first decent job that came his way. My dilemma is that *I'm* the one who has to put up with you being a miserable cow all day—he doesn't."

Kayli swiftly turned to face him, her mouth gaping open in surprise.

"The road! Keep your eyes on the road!" he shouted, his eyes widening in fear.

"Stop dropping frigging statements like that and let me drive then. Bloody hell! Anyone would think I've been a mardy cow to be around lately. I haven't, have I?"

"Do you mind if I answer that when you're not driving? It might be safer, for both of us."

"Seriously, Dave? Is that what you think, or are you just winding me up?"

He refused to answer until she'd pulled into the hospital car park a few minutes later. She found a space tucked away in the corner and swivelled in her seat to face him. "Answer me."

"I was winding you up. See? I rest my case: you're super sensitive, at least you have been over the past few weeks. Since Mark went off on his travels, shall we say."

They exited the car and walked towards the main entrance of the huge building. "I had no idea I'd been so bad. Why didn't you say something sooner?"

"Nah, you haven't really been that bad." He held up his finger and forefinger, showing a little gap in between. "Just a soupçon."

Kayli laughed. "Where the heck did that word come from?"

"I heard it on TV last night, promised myself I'd use it in a sentence today."

"You challenge yourself to do things like that? And you think *I* have problems?"

They approached the young blonde woman with the friendly smile on reception, and Kayli flashed her ID. "We're looking for the A&E department. That is where the air ambulance takes casualties, yes?"

"That's correct. Follow the red line around to your right."

"Thanks very much."

They did as they were instructed and walked through the swinging doors of the Accident and Emergency Department a few minutes later. Another reception area was in front of them, where a young man was on duty behind the high counter.

"Hello there. How can I help?"

Kayli showed the man her ID. "We were called to the scene of an accident this morning, and the air ambulance just brought the woman in. Are we in the right place?"

The elevator on the right pinged, and the doors flew open to reveal the doctor and a couple of porters who were pushing the stretcher with the woman from the crash.

"Never mind, I see that we are." Kayli rushed towards the doctor. "We're here when you get five minutes, Doctor."

"Let me get the X-Ray organised and hand her over to the relevant specialist, and I'll come back and have a chat with you. Have you informed her next of kin?"

"Yes, her boyfriend is on his way. We'll see you soon," she called after him as he and his team rushed the stretcher through the hallway.

Kayli and Dave paced the area, waiting for news. A tall, good-looking man in his late twenties walked towards Kayli. His brown hair was messed up as if it hadn't been combed in days. He looked anxious, as if he were on the lookout for someone. "Lincoln James?"

He shook her hand and nodded. "That's right. How is Carmen?"

"We've yet to find out the extent of her injuries. They're in there assessing her now and will be sending her to the X-Ray department soon."

"They must have some clue how bad she is."

"It's a waiting game. Why don't we take a seat, and I'll ask you a few questions, if that's all right?"

"Right now? My mind is all over the place. I didn't get in until four this morning, and you woke me up with this devastating news. I'm not trying to be awkward, Inspector, but can you give me a break until I've had a chance to let this all sink in?"

"Very well. However, the quicker we have a chat, the sooner we can get on with our investigation."

He sighed heavily and ran a hand through his hair. "Okay, you win. What do you need to know?"

"Why was your girlfriend out late last night?"

"She went out for a celebratory drink with a couple of friends while I was at work."

"Can you give me the friends' phone numbers?"

"No. I don't have their numbers, but their names are Dawn Finch and Sonia Lewis, if that will help?"

"Any idea where they work?"

"At a salon in town. One is a hairdresser, and the other is a beautician, I believe. Don't quote me on that. That's classed as girly things, and I tend to switch off when they're over at our place, discussing such matters. Sorry, I'm waffling."

"You're doing fine. Dave, can you see what Donna can come up with, please?"

Dave walked a few yards away to place the call. Kayli smiled at the young man, whose brow was pulled into a concerned frown. "I take it you and Carmen live together?"

"Yes, that's right. We're due to get married next year ... at least we were ... crap, I should ring Jacky, her sister."

"Yes, that would be a good idea. Does Jacky live locally?"

"Fifteen minutes away. She should be able to get here. She's a housewife, has a toddler at home. On second thoughts, maybe it will be impossible for her to come."

"Can you ring her? If she prefers, I can organise a patrol car to pick her up and bring her in."

"No, I think she'd hate that. Her neighbours are prone to gossiping, and she'd detest being the talk of the street if a police car pulled up outside her house."

"Please ring her, then we'll chat afterwards."

"You want her here in case Carmen dies, don't you? It's worse than you've let on."

"Truthfully? I haven't got a clue. Can you tell Jacky it's urgent she gets here without scaring her? I think that would be best."

"I'll try. Jesus, my mind is all over the place ... what if?"

Kayli placed a hand on his arm. "Why don't I ring her? Maybe it would be better coming from me."

He nodded, punched the number into his phone, and handed it to her. After three rings, a woman answered, "Lincoln?"

"Hello there. You're right, this is Lincoln's phone. I'm DI Bright of the Avon and Somerset Constabulary, Jacky."

"What? Has something happened to Lincoln? Why are you calling me and not my sister?"

"Sorry, no, Lincoln is fine. He's with me here at the hospital."

"Hospital? Then everything is not okay. What's going on, Inspector?"

"Can you come to the hospital? I'm afraid your sister has been involved in an accident."

"What? When? How? Is it bad?"

She could hear the woman bustling around, as if gathering things together, then keys jangling.

"The doctors are assessing her now."

A door slammed, and Kayli heard a child chattering, asking where they were going. "I'm getting in the car now."

"Brilliant. Please drive carefully. We're in the Accident and Emergency Department. See you soon."

"Thank you." The line went dead.

Kayli handed the phone back to Lincoln. He slipped it into his jacket pocket. "Why haven't the doctors come to see us yet? I just know it's bad news."

"Not necessarily. It must be difficult if she's unconscious and can't tell them where it hurts. Is it usual for Carmen to travel alone at night?"

"Yes, why?"

"I just wondered. Does your girlfriend drink alcohol?"

"No. She never touches the stuff. She's always said that she can have a good time without getting pissed—sorry, drunk."

"I see." Kayli smiled.

"You think the accident was her fault?"

"It's too early to tell yet. We have accident specialists looking over the site now. They'll give us their report in the next day or so, I should imagine. I have to tell you that Carmen went through one of the barriers on the main road."

"How is that even possible? Those things are supposed to prevent that kind of thing from happening, aren't they?"

"Like I say, there is a specialist team at the site. I'm hoping they'll be able to make a proper assessment of how the accident occurred soon."

"What about a blowout?"

"I took a quick look around the car, and the tyres appeared to be intact."

Dave rejoined them. "I've spoken to both Dawn and Sonia and arranged to meet with them this afternoon. I told them that Carmen is in hospital. They were really upset, as you can imagine."

"Maybe they'll be able to shed some light on things later," Lincoln said.

"Lincoln, I have to ask if Carmen has mentioned if someone has been acting suspicious around her lately? Or perhaps she's noticed someone following her?"

He fell silent as he contemplated her question, then he shook his head. "I don't recall her mentioning anything along those lines. Do you think this was intentional?"

"Again, I really can't tell at this point. I just prefer to ask these kinds of questions now rather than later."

Kayli heard heels clicking on the tiled floor behind them, then Dave nudged her arm. She turned to see a pretty brunette holding a toddler in her arms rushing towards them. When she reached them, Lincoln attempted to kiss her on the cheek, but she took a step back. Kayli thought it strange that the woman should try to dodge the affection under the circumstances.

"What's going on, Lincoln? Have you seen her?" the woman demanded harshly.

He shook his head. "No. The doctors are still checking her over. No one has come to see us yet."

Kayli offered her hand and introduced herself and Dave. "You must be Jacky? We spoke on the phone. Why don't we try and find a family room where we can wait? Dave, can you do that for me?"

Dave marched down the hallway and spoke to the receptionist. Jacky pulled a dummy out of her pocket and gave it to her child while they waited. Dave beckoned them a few seconds later. They all followed him down the hallway into a square room with several comfortable chairs positioned along each of the walls.

Jacky sat down and settled her child in her arms. She rummaged around in her bag and pulled out a bottle of milk, which the child grasped hungrily.

"Are you all right talking in front of your son?" Kayli asked.

"Yes, he'll be fine. What happened? Is Carmen very bad? I guess she must be if they haven't let Lincoln in to see her yet."

"Carmen's car was the only one involved in the crash. She hit one of the barriers and tumbled down the embankment. The car landed on its roof. The fire brigade had to cut her from the wreckage."

"What? How could that have happened?" Jacky asked, looking confused.

"Accident investigators are evaluating the scene as we speak. I hope to have their report on my desk within a few days. When was the last time you spoke to your sister?"

"Yesterday. She rings every day to see how I am. My husband ran out on me a couple of months ago, and I've not been coping very well."

Maybe that's why Jacky gave Lincoln the cold shoulder when she arrived. "Sorry to hear that. Did your sister mention anything about anyone being an annoyance to her?" Kayli watched her reaction carefully as her eyes drifted over to Lincoln, who was standing guard at the door, waiting for the doctor to arrive. "Jacky?"

"No, not that I can think of."

Kayli didn't force the issue, but she felt that Jacky was holding something back regarding Lincoln. "What kind of mood was your sister in when she called you yesterday?"

"Carmen was as upbeat as she always is. She had a right to be happy too. She's just gained a promotion at work. I believe that's why she was out celebrating last night with Dawn and Sonia. My God, she wasn't drinking, was she?"

"According to Lincoln, she doesn't drink."

"That's right. But this promotion was huge for her. She was up against some stiff competition, and she was handed the post against all the odds. She might have thought what the heck, this kind of thing only happens in a blue moon and had a tipple to celebrate with the girls. Have you spoken to them yet?"

"My partner has made arrangements for us to see them this afternoon. I think it's unlikely that your sister would change her drinking habits in order to celebrate."

"You're right. I can't imagine her doing it, either, if I'm honest. I was trying to think of an explanation why she would have come off the road. And another car definitely wasn't involved?" Jacky asked, stroking the head of her child as he drank his milk.

"We're not sure. There wasn't another car at the scene, but that doesn't necessarily mean to say that another vehicle wasn't involved initially. Maybe they hit her and thought they'd be in trouble if they stuck around."

"Aren't there any cameras in that area? Can't you check them?"

"That's one of the first things we'll do once we get back to the station. I just want to see how Carmen is first. When she wakes up, hopefully she'll be able to tell us how the accident occurred."

"A doctor is coming!" Lincoln shouted, reaching for the door.

"Hello, everyone. I'm Dr. Enright. I understand you're Carmen Drinkwater's family?"

Jacky nodded. "I'm her sister."

The doctor smiled briefly. "It's not looking good, I'm afraid."

Kayli's hand automatically covered Jacky's. "What's wrong with Carmen, Doctor?"

"There was a delay, but it's sorted now. The porter is on his way to take her down to X-Ray. My initial diagnosis is that she possibly has a ruptured spleen because there is extensive bruising to her stomach, indicating internal bleeding. We'll need to carry out an MRI scan to verify that. She also likely has several broken ribs, which may have punctured a lung. The scans will tell us what other damage there is inside."

Jacky burst into tears. Kayli slung an arm around her shoulders to comfort her.

"What does that mean, Doctor? Ruptured spleen?" Lincoln asked.

"Well, it means that Carmen could have a lot of internal bleeding. She'll need an emergency operation. We're assembling the theatre staff now, and once we have the X-Ray and MRI results, we'll be better prepared to put those injuries right. I wanted to bring you up-to-date before we go any further."

"Can we see her?" Jacky asked, sniffling.

"Only briefly before she's taken down. I have to warn you that your sister is badly bruised and has several cuts on her face."

"I don't care what she looks like. I just need to see my sister."

The doctor nodded. "Very well, if you'd like to come with me. It'll be a quick visit, okay?"

"Why don't I look after your son," Dave volunteered.

An uncertain look crossed Jacky's face, but Kayli nodded. "He'll be fine with Dave. He has a son around the same age."

Dave sat down in the chair beside her, and Jacky passed her son over to him gently. He was still consuming his bottle and didn't appear to mind the transition.

"We won't be long," Kayli called over her shoulder as she, Lincoln, and Jacky left the room. She noticed Jacky's breathing had become erratic. "Hey, you need to calm down before you see her. She might be unconscious, but I've heard patients in that state are still aware of what is going on around them."

Jacky inhaled and exhaled several times before they entered triage. She gasped when she saw her sister, lying unresponsively, except for the expansion of her chest now and again, on one of the trolleys. She was connected to a couple of drips.

"Are you all right? Be brave for Carmen's sake," Kayli said, hooking her hand under Jacky's arm to support and guide her towards her sister. "Lincoln, how are you holding up?"

"I'm fine. I think. Crap, she's really been through the mire."

Kayli nodded. "Literally. Carmen's car was found overturned, the roof caved in. She'd been there for several hours."

"How dreadful! I'm so relieved someone found her before ..." Jacky's voice faltered.

"We have no idea how long she was like that."

A couple of nurses smiled and stood away from the trolley so the group could get closer. Jacky laid her hand over her sister's bloody hand. "Don't give up, Carmen. Please come back to us. We need you."

Lincoln stood on the other side and leaned down to kiss his girlfriend's cheek. His tears dripped onto Carmen's face. "Hello, beautiful. Stick with us. I love you."

Kayli thought it strange that Jacky should stiffen beside her when Lincoln voiced the sentiment. She sensed there was more to this situation than met the eye.

A porter appeared along with Dr. Enright. "I'm sorry, but they're ready for her now."

"One sec, Doc," Kayli leaned over Carmen and touched her hand. "We'll be here when you wake up."

The monitor began to beep loudly. Carmen's eyes flew open, her tongue moistened her lips, and she whispered two words, "Baby ... bike."

The next thing Kayli knew, she was being yanked out of the way by the doctor. His staff had gathered around the trolley again.

A nurse hurried them to one side. "Maybe it would be better if you went back to the family room. We'll call you when we can."

Kayli nodded. "She's right. Come on, Jacky, Lincoln. Let's leave them to ..." Her voice trailed off as a long high-pitched tone filled the room.

"What's going on?" Jacky shouted as the doctor walked towards them.

"Please, leave us to try and work on her."

"She's dead, isn't she?" Jacky screeched.

Kayli took control of the situation, forcing Lincoln and Jacky into the hallway. "Come on, guys. We're in the way. Let them do their job."

Ten minutes later, Dr. Enright emerged from the swinging doors, his expression very sombre. He shook his head. "I'm sorry. We did everything we could to try and save her. Carmen's injuries proved to be too much for her body to handle in the end."

Jacky cried out and collapsed to her knees. She began to rock backwards and forwards. Kayli kneeled on the floor and tried to gather the woman in her arms, but Jacky shrugged her off. "Why? Why Carmen? She was the sweetest person ever to walk this earth. What am I going to do without her?"

Lincoln stepped forward to comfort Jacky. She recoiled from his touch as if he'd prodded her with a red-hot poker. "Jacky, don't do this. Carmen wouldn't want you to be upset like this."

"Sod off. What you said back there repulsed me. You didn't love her. You pretended to love her, but I saw through you. She was too wrapped up in you to see what you're truly like. Get out of here. You have no right to be here."

Kayli's gaze swiftly moved between Jacky and Lincoln. "What's this about, Jacky? Is there something I should know?"

"She's grieving, Inspector, has no idea what she's saying," Lincoln stated heatedly.

"I know exactly what I'm saying. Get out of here, you waste of space."

Lincoln shrugged. "I refuse to stay where I'm not wanted. I'll do my grieving on my own."

"We'll be in touch in a day or two, Lincoln," Kayli called out after him.

"You need to dig deep on that one, Inspector. There's more to him than his cocky smile and glistening white teeth."

"I'll be sure to check his past thoroughly. I'm so sorry about Carmen. Here, let me help you stand up."

Once Jacky was standing, her legs almost gave way beneath her again. Kayli hooked her arm through Jacky's and guided her back to the family room. Dave looked up expectantly when they appeared in the doorway. Kayli shook her head. He looked mortified.

"I think Jacky could do with a cuddle from her son." Kayli deposited Jacky into the seat beside Dave, and he handed her son back to her.

"I'm sorry for your loss, Jacky," Dave uttered, stroking the baby's face with his finger.

She buried her face into her son's neck and sobbed.

CHAPTER TWO

Kayli felt emotional on the ride back to the station. Dave had agreed to drive, giving her time to reflect on what had happened at the hospital. Jacky had insisted that she wanted to remain close to her sister for the next few hours. Kayli understood how she felt and didn't try to dissuade her.

She fished her mobile out of her jacket pocket and dialled her sister-in-law's number. "Hi, Annabelle, it's me. How are you?"

"Hey, you. I'm surviving, just. How are you?"

"I could do with a chat and a hug from my favourite nephew, if you must know. Fancy a takeaway tonight?"

There was a slight pause before her sister-in-law replied, "Go on then. Although I have to warn you, I haven't got much of an appetite at the moment."

"That makes two of us. We can pick at our food together. I'll just get the one main portion of chicken then and lots of veg. How's that?"

"Sounds ideal. Nothing too greasy."

"Trust me. See you around six thirty. That won't be too late for Bobby, will it?"

"It should be fine. I'll put him down for a nap this afternoon."

"Brilliant. See you later."

"Kayli ... thanks for thinking of me."

"Always, lovely." Guilt draped around her shoulders. Since Giles and Mark had been away, she'd only had the chance to visit Annabelle once due to her busy schedule.

"Are you all right?" Dave asked, pulling the car into the station's car park.

"I'm fine. Just feeling a little lost right now. It's hard to explain, really."

"I'm always here if you need a chat, and Luke's always around if you need a cuddle. I know it's not the same as cuddling your flesh and blood, but he's a good stand-in."

Kayli smiled at her partner's generous offer. "I know. I appreciate that, matey. I should go round and see Annabelle more, though. She's stuck at home all day with only Bobby to keep her company."

"Not the brightest idea your brother has ever had, is it?" Dave said as they left the car.

"I'm beginning to think the same thing."

Waiting for them at the top of the stairs was DCI Sandra Davis. "Morning, you two. I'd like a word with you in my office, Inspector." She turned on her heel and called out, "Now!"

Dave grimaced. "Someone sounds annoyed. You better not keep Frosty Knickers waiting."

Kayli stifled a laugh. "Did you have to say that? How am I going to keep a straight face now whilst standing in the line of fire? I wonder what's eating her. I'm not aware of doing anything wrong."

"It looked pretty serious to me. Good luck."

They separated, and Kayli had trouble keeping her legs from shaking as she walked towards the DCI's office. Fiona, the DCI's secretary, smiled broadly at her when she entered the room. The DCI's office door was open. "I've been summoned, should I go straight in?" she whispered.

"You should. Good luck."

"Crap! Do I need it?"

Fiona shrugged and winked at her.

Bollocks! What the hell is this all about? She rapped her knuckles on the door and gingerly poked her head into the office. "You wanted to see me, ma'am?"

"Stop dilly-dallying in the blasted doorway and take a seat, Inspector."

"Sorry. Have I done something wrong?" Kayli asked once she was seated. She crossed then uncrossed her legs, agitated to be sitting before her superior.

"Why is that always the first question you ask? My reply, as always, is I don't know, have you?"

"Touché, ma'am."

DCI Davis leaned back in her chair and clasped her hands together in front of her. "Perhaps you can answer me a question."

Kayli tilted her head. "I'll do my best. What is it?"

38

"Why wasn't I told about your personal situation?"

"I'm not with you, ma'am. My personal situation? In what respect?"

The DCI shook her head, an expression of annoyance settling on her face. "Stop with the bullshit. You know exactly what I'm talking about. Your other half going off to Lord knows where."

"I didn't know I had to report my partner's every move to you, ma'am. It's not like it's affecting my job."

The DCI raised an eyebrow. "Isn't it? Look at you! You've lost a hell of a lot of weight. Did you think I wouldn't notice?"

"Have I? And that's your concern because?"

"Don't smart-mouth me, Inspector. It doesn't become you. Am I that much of an ogre that you find it impossible to confide in me?"

"Not at all. I wasn't aware that it was compulsory to tell you when Mark went away. I'm at a loss to know what I've done wrong."

DCI Davis exhaled an exasperated breath. "You haven't done anything wrong. It would have been nice if you'd made me aware of the situation, so I could monitor it. That's all."

"*Monitor* it? What's there to monitor, ma'am?" Kayli fidgeted in her seat some more.

"The fact that you've lost a lot of weight and look gaunt—unhealthy, if you like. Now are you getting my drift, Inspector? Obviously not, by the perplexed look on your face. Unhealthy means that you're lacking in sleep and prone to making mistakes on the job. Has that clarified things enough for you?"

"With respect, ma'am, that's utter bollocks. I have gone about my duties in the same way I always have. Nothing has changed to me, unless you're saying that you've noticed a decline in my abilities to carry out my job properly."

"I'm not saying I've noticed any such thing. This meeting is about preventing the rot before it sets in."

"I have no intention of letting either you or my team down, ma'am. I'm actually offended that thought should even enter your mind."

DCI Davis exhaled loudly again. "It hasn't. I'm doing something about it before it does. When is Mark due back?"

"At the end of this week. Five days and counting."

"Good. Why on earth did he take such a dangerous job in the first place?"

Kayli shrugged. She'd asked herself that question a hundred times over the past two weeks. "He tried to get a job in this country, but no one could be bothered to employ him. He was getting low about not being able to contribute to the household expenses and grabbed the opportunity to make some decent money when it was presented to him on a plate by my brother."

"I see. Does this mean that your brother is also tangled up in this mess?"

Kayli unfolded her legs and leaned forward. "I'd hardly call it a 'mess', ma'am."

"You have your opinions, and I have mine on the subject. All I know is what I'm seeing in front of me and the effect this role he's taken is having on you and your well-being."

"I'm fine. There's no need for you to be concerned. I've just made arrangements to go round my sister-in-law's tonight for a take-away, if you must know. That's sure to put a couple of pounds on."

"You could do with putting a couple of stone on, not pounds, Inspector," DCI Davis retorted sharply.

"Nonsense. How on earth would I be able to chase criminals then?"

"You delegate. Get Dave Chaplin to do it instead."

Kayli fell silent. She knew there was no point in arguing with the DCI, who'd been known to give the most stubborn mule a good run for its money.

"I see you followed up on an accident report first thing this morning. Do you believe it warrants an investigation?"

Relieved the subject had changed, Kayli shrugged. "Very early days. I've yet to have it confirmed by the investigation team overseeing things at the site, but I don't think it was a mere accident. I've just come from the hospital; unfortunately, the victim has lost her life."

"A murder enquiry then? I'm sorry to hear the victim has died. Any suspects yet?"

"Give me a chance, ma'am. There's something dubious about the boyfriend—not sure what—but I'll get my team digging into his background now. She was out socialising with two friends last night; I'm due to question the women this afternoon. They might have encountered something unsavoury that led to Miss Drinkwater's death."

"Okay. You better get on with things. Keep me up-to-date with your progress."

"Will do." Kayli rose from her chair and walked towards the door.

"And Inspector, I suggest you have a good chat with that fella of yours when he returns. Let him know exactly what turmoil he is inflicting on you in his absence."

"It's not going to happen, ma'am. I refuse to dictate how I think he should be running his life."

DCI Davis's eyes rolled up to the ceiling before she dropped her head and pulled some paperwork in front of her. "Shut the door on your way out."

On the way back to the incident room, Kayli continually kicked herself. *Why? Why did I have to retaliate like that? Why didn't I just accept what she said and get on with it?*

"I need coffee, preferably intravenously," she insisted, rushing towards the vending machine.

Dave laughed. "That bad, eh?"

"Think of the worst scenario you can think of and multiply it by a thousand," she said, exaggerating.

The three members of the team all looked at each other with dread in their eyes.

"Anything we can do to help?" Dave asked.

"Nope. Just stand by me and don't question me about my personal life because I'm liable to put you in your place like I stupidly just did to the DCI. I'll be sulking in my office if you need me, for the next five minutes, anyway." *Stop wallowing! I need to forget what just happened and get on with the case ASAP.* "In the meantime, Donna, can you dig up everything you can regarding Lincoln James, the victim's boyfriend? Something isn't ringing true with him, and I want to know what that is."

"I'm looking into it now, boss. I've not found anything so far."

"What do you want me to do?" Dave sat forward in his chair.

"We need to go and interview the two friends soon. Maybe you can try and pick up Carmen's car on the CCTV footage, or at least make a start on the search before we set off. We need to know if anyone was following her last night. She said two words to me before she passed away: 'baby' and 'bike'. She could have been hinting that she swerved to avoid hitting a bike. I doubt if she meant a baby was on the road, but who knows?"

"Gotcha. I'll make a start with Graeme, unless you want him to do something else?"

"No, that's fine with me. Give me ten minutes, all right?" Kayli walked into her office. She opened the window to let some fresh air into the small office, but closed it rapidly when a strong gust of wind snatched the windowpane from her hand. *God, how I hate the winter! I envy you one thing in your new role, Mark—at least you've got sunshine where you are.* She spent the next ten minutes going over some paperwork head office had sent through the internal mail system, but she found herself scratching her head. None of it seemed to make much sense. Maybe she was more distracted about Mark than she was prepared to admit. Perhaps Dave and DCI Davis were right. Or maybe Carmen's death was the problem. Kayli hated it when things weren't cut and dried at the beginning of a case. After shoving the papers in the in-tray again, she downed her coffee and left the office. "Found anything yet, Donna?"

"No, boss. Nothing official like a police record so far."

"I kind of suspected that, especially as he runs a bar. He'd need to be squeaky clean to obtain his liquor licence in the first place."

"That's a good point. I'll keep digging."

"Are you ready, Dave? You can tell me about your progress with the footage en route."

He slipped on his jacket and followed her out of the room and down the stairs to the car.

Once they were on the road, Dave told her, "We haven't found anything yet. Mind you, we're a little in the dark as to where to look, because we have no idea where she set off from. I hope the two friends can fill in the blanks of what route she took."

"Let's hope so. I have to say, I'm not looking forward to sharing the news that Carmen didn't make it. You said they were devastated that she was in the accident. Lord knows what their reaction is going to be after hearing the news of her death."

They parked in the multi-storey car park close to Cabot Circus where Dawn's Beautification Salon was based.

"Crikey, this looks a bit swish," Dave muttered.

As they walked through the door, a mixture of smells hit Kayli's nose. The pungent smell of bleach or peroxide challenged the smell of nail lacquer being applied by one of the assistants sitting in the near corner of the room.

A girl with bright-pink hair was standing behind the small desk. "Hello there. Do you have an appointment?"

"We have a meeting with Dawn and Sonia."

The girl turned and shouted above the din of the hairdryers. "Dawn, there's someone to see you."

A pretty brunette with wavy brown hair looked over her shoulder, glared at the receptionist, and smiled at Kayli. "Can you give me five minutes to finish off Mrs. Tucker?"

"Of course. Maybe we could chat with Sonia first?" Kayli shouted back.

"Good idea. Sam, show them through to the staffroom. Sonia is on her break."

"Like to come this way." The girl smiled and set off in her high heels. Her shocking-pink tights matched her hair, reminding Kayli of a character from the Trolls movie, and she was wearing the shortest denim miniskirt Kayli had ever seen.

Kayli turned sideways to see Dave's eyes homed in on the girl's shapely backside, which earned him a jab in the ribs.

"What?" he mouthed with all the innocence of a hormone-rampant ten-year-old.

Kayli tutted and shook her head. *Men! You're the same the world over.*

Sam pushed open the door to a relatively small room. "Sonia, I have the two police officers to see you."

Sonia leapt out of her chair and began tidying her lunch cartons away. "Excuse the mess. Come in and take a seat."

"No need to tidy up on our account. I'm DI Kayli Bright, and this is my partner, Dave Chaplin. Would you rather we spoke to you and Dawn at the same time, or are you happy to speak to us alone?"

"I need to get back to work soon. I have a client due in ten minutes, sorry."

"No problem. Can we sit down?"

"Please do. How's Carmen doing? It was such a shock to hear she was in hospital." Sonia ran a hand over her face and gathered her blonde hair into a ponytail with a coloured band.

Kayli inhaled a breath. "Oh dear, it's extremely hard for me to tell you this, but unfortunately, Carmen died a few hours ago."

Sonia's first reaction was to let her mouth drop open, then she covered her face with her hands and sobbed. "No, not Carmen. There must be some mistake."

Tears misted Kayli's vision. "I'm sorry. I was there when she passed away. The doctors did everything they could to save her, but the internal injuries she had suffered during the crash proved to be too much in the end."

The door flew open, and Dawn entered the room. She took one look at Sonia and rushed to her side. "Sonia, what's wrong? Oh shit! It's not ...? She's not ...?"

Sonia looked at her friend and nodded as fresh tears slid down her face. She whispered, "She's gone, Dawn."

Dawn, forgetting she was wearing a mid-thigh dress, collapsed on the floor beside her friend and buried her face in her hands. "How could this be? Not Carmen—please tell me this is some kind of cruel joke?"

"I'm so sorry. I wish I could tell you it was a mistake, but it isn't. She suffered a ruptured spleen in the accident, and the internal bleeding proved to be too significant in the end. There was nothing the medical staff could do to save her."

The two women hugged each other, sobbing as more tears fell. It was uncomfortable for both Dave and Kayli to witness, but the women's distraught reactions were understandable.

"Look," Kayli said, "would you rather we came back another time, once this news has sunk in?"

Dawn released her friend and shook her head. "No. Your partner said this was a suspicious accident. You need to ask your questions now to get the case going. Isn't that how this works? By suspicious are you suggesting Carmen was murdered?"

"We do need to ask our questions, but we're also keen not to come across as insensitive. We appreciate how difficult this news must be for you to swallow. We wouldn't be in such a rush if we were dealing with a normal accident."

"Are you all right to answer some questions, Sonia?" Dawn asked.

Sonia sniffled. "I think so."

"Tell me to stop if it all becomes overwhelming for either of you."

The two women nodded. Dawn stood up and moved a spare chair into position beside Sonia, and they held each other's hands.

"First of all, we need to establish where you were last night."

"We were having a drink at the Jolly Roger pub on the outskirts of Sea Mills. We were celebrating Carmen's promotion," Dawn said, her voice catching a little.

"That's very sad. I have to ask, did this celebration involve alcohol?"

"Definitely not. Sonia and I both drank, but Carmen refused to." Dawn's gaze drifted to the floor.

"Dawn, is there something you're not telling us?"

Tears cascaded down her cheeks. She swallowed hard and grasped her friend's hand tighter until her knuckles grew white. "She was pregnant."

Sonia turned her head sharply towards Dawn. "No! Why didn't either of you tell me? How could you keep that news from me?"

"I'm sorry. Carmen wanted to wait until the twelve weeks were up before she started spreading the word. I guessed, and she found it impossible to deny it when I tackled her about it a few weeks ago. I found her being sick in the ladies' loo on a night out."

"I can't believe it ... now she and the baby are ..." Sonia withdrew her hand from Dawn's to cover her face again, then bawled.

"Please forgive me, Sonia. I was only abiding by Carmen's wishes. Please don't let us fall out about this."

Sonia released her hands and looked her friend in the eye. "I feel betrayed."

Kayli coughed and reached over to touch Sonia's knee. "I know it must feel that way, but if Carmen asked Dawn to keep it a secret ..."

"I'm not blaming Dawn. I would never do that. Sorry, just ignore me. Go on." She plucked a tissue from the box sitting on the table and blew her nose.

Kayli nodded. "Did anyone approach you girls during the night? You know, making a nuisance of themselves, perhaps?"

Dawn frowned. "No. Not that I can recollect."

Sonia gasped. "You think someone followed her?"

"We're merely trying to form a picture in our minds at present," Kayli said.

"No. Nothing like that occurred. We had a genuinely nice evening, just the three of us," Dawn replied.

"And did you all leave at the same time?"

"No. Sonia and I stayed behind to finish our drinks. I went out to the car park to see Carmen to her car and then returned to the pub."

"What time was that?"

Dawn chewed her lip. "Around eleven, I suppose."

"I see, and do you remember seeing anyone else in the car park, acting suspicious?"

"There was no one out there." Dawn thought for a second then clarified, "Or if there was, I didn't see them."

"That leads me to ask how Lincoln and Carmen's relationship was. Were they happy? I got the impression that Lincoln didn't know about the baby at the hospital, or if he did, he never mentioned it."

"Carmen hadn't told him. That's why I ran after her—to ask if she'd told Lincoln. She said she wanted him to get used to the idea of her promotion before she hit him with the news about the baby."

"Bloody hell, Lincoln didn't know, either?" Sonia said, sounding mortified.

"No. See? You weren't the only one, love." Dawn rubbed her friend's hand.

"Ouch, poor Lincoln. Their relationship was good apart from that one secret, though?" Kayli asked.

Dawn shrugged. "Yes, I think Carmen would have told us if there had been any problems. Mind you, they had different shift patterns so rarely spent much time together. Maybe that was the secret of their success."

"Maybe you're right," Kayli said, her own situation coming to mind for an instant. "Could there have been another reason why Carmen hadn't informed Lincoln of the pregnancy?"

"I'm not with you," Dawn said.

"I appreciate they worked opposite shifts, but did Carmen ever mention that everything wasn't as it seemed with their relationship?"

Sonia clicked her fingers. "Hey, you remember a few weeks back? She said that she wasn't sure if something was wrong with Lincoln. Wasn't it around the time she told him she'd had her interview for the promotion?"

"Yes, I remember, now that you've mentioned it. She said he was a little distant for some reason. When she asked what was wrong, he refused to tell her. He insisted everything was okay. Maybe deep down that's why she hadn't told him about the baby," Dawn said, running a hand around her chin.

Kayli looked over at Dave, who was jotting everything down in his notebook. "Interesting. Thanks for that. Do you know if everything was going well at work for Carmen, aside from her promotion, that is? Maybe she told you about a colleague showing interest in her that wasn't reciprocated? Something along those lines?"

Dawn shook her head. "Not that I can think of. What about you, Sonia?"

"Nope, I can't recall her ever mentioning her colleagues except in passing. I couldn't tell you any of their names, anyway."

"All right, we'll drop by to see her boss, make sure that really is the case. Again, she might not have shared with either of you if there was a problem at work."

"I hope it was an accident and your assumption is wrong. I'd hate to think someone deliberately had it in for Carmen," Dawn said, shaking her head.

"We don't want to rule anything out at this early stage of the enquiry. Did Carmen have an ex-boyfriend?"

"Apart from Wayne—she finished with him about eight years ago—there's been no one except Lincoln."

"Wayne? Can you think of his surname?"

Dawn thought it over for a second then nodded. "Nutkins, I believe. He no longer lives in this country. He moved to Australia ... come to think of it, that's why they split up. He wanted her to go with him, but there was no way she would have left her family and friends. She was really close to her sister, Jacky. My God, does Jacky know?"

"Yes. Lincoln called her to come to the hospital, and she was there when Carmen passed away."

"I'm glad she wasn't alone at the end," Sonia said, dabbing at her red eyes.

"Me too," Dawn agreed.

"Okay, ladies. I think we've taken up enough of your time now. We're sorry that we had to meet under such dire circumstances and really do appreciate the information you have given us to get the investigation going." Kayli rose from her chair.

Dave tucked his notebook away and followed her out the door.

At the entrance of the salon, Kayli shook Dawn's and Sonia's hands before leaving.

"Please, if this wasn't an accident, Inspector, find the person responsible for our dear friend's death," Dawn said tearfully.

"We're going to do our very best. My team will be on top of their game to bring Carmen and her friends and family the justice they deserve. Goodbye, ladies."

They were halfway to the car before either of them spoke.

"You think the boyfriend has something to do with this?" Dave asked.

Kayli tutted. "To be honest, I really don't have a clue, Dave. But I'm going to give it my all to find out. Maybe it was an accident after all. Nothing is really screaming at me to arrest Lincoln and bring him in for questioning yet."

Kayli's mobile rang. The name of the pathologist on their patch was highlighted on the tiny screen. "Hi, Naomi. I was going to ring you later."

"Hi, Kayli. Thought I better touch base to tell you that I've taken delivery of Carmen Drinkwater's body. I'll be performing the post-mortem on her this afternoon."

"I'm glad she'll be in your safe hands, Naomi. We're unsure at this point what we're dealing with. There's a chance she might be a murder victim, or she could have been involved in a nasty accident, but that's doubtful as there were no other cars at the scene, not that that makes any difference nowadays. We could be looking at a joyrider incident. I know, I'm prattling on. Just trying to tell you how it is."

Naomi laughed. "Okay, message received and understood."

"And Naomi, we believe Carmen was pregnant."

"Damn! Hate it when that bloody happens. I'll get back to you with the results as soon as humanly possible."

"I appreciate it. Thanks."

Dave looked at her expectantly after Kayli hung up. "Naomi just informed me that she's going to start the PM on Carmen this afternoon."

"I gathered that. Does she think it looks suspicious?"

"Not sure. I detected something in her voice but can't put my finger on what. I thought I better warn her that Carmen was pregnant, though. Let's get back to see how the others are doing."

When they arrived, Graeme called Kayli over to his desk. He pointed to his monitor at a motorbike. "Where is this, Graeme?"

"On the B4054, about a mile from the crash."

She patted him on the shoulder. "That's excellent work, Graeme. Carmen's friends have now confirmed that they spent the evening in a pub on the edge of Sea Mills, the Jolly Roger. Can you try to find out if the bike was seen in that area around elevenish when Carmen left? It might tell us if someone was stalking her or if the bike is a

48

red herring, although why would it be one of the last words to ever leave her lips if there was no significance?"

"Leave it with me. Now that I know a time and location, it should be easy enough to find out."

Kayli left her team and spent the rest of the afternoon in her office. When she emerged later, Graeme reluctantly shook his head. "Nothing yet, boss. I'll look over the footage again in the morning with fresh eyes, if that's all right with you?"

"That's just what I was about to suggest, Graeme. Okay, gang, let's call it a day and start with renewed vigour first thing in the morning."

The team switched off their computers, tucked their chairs under their desks, then left the room as a group.

Kayli's stomach began to flutter. She was excited about seeing Annabelle and Bobby.

"Have fun at your sister-in-law's!" Dave shouted before he jumped into his car.

Kayli pulled up outside the Chinese takeaway close to Annabelle's around fifteen minutes later. She studied the menu carefully, sourcing a meal they could share that wouldn't be too greasy, and decided that chicken with cashew nuts would be an ideal choice. She ordered a portion of noodles and broccoli and concluded that would be enough for both of them to share, thinking that Bobby would already have been fed.

The order took twenty minutes to complete. She fished out her phone and dialled Annabelle. "I'm on my way with a steaming food package."

"Great, I'll get the plates ready. See you soon."

CHAPTER THREE

Annabelle and Bobby were waiting at the door to greet her when she pulled up outside their home. The weather was definitely turning wintry, and a fine drizzle was beginning to fall. "Yuck, I hate the rain. Still, I suppose it's better than snow." She kissed her sister-in-law on the cheek and ruffled her nephew's hair. "Crikey, he's grown since I last saw him at the family barbeque a few weeks ago."

"Come in out of the rain. Do you think so? It's hard to tell when you're with him as much as I am. He's crawling a lot faster, I'll say that. He's like a bloody greyhound out of the traps some days."

"Can I hold him?"

"Of course. We'll do a swap. I'll dish up while you have a cuddle. How does that sound?"

Kayli handed Annabelle the bag of food and took Bobby from his mother's arms. The toddler didn't kick up a fuss like he usually did, which pleased Kayli. Maybe he was finally getting used to her. They went through to the lounge, and Kayli sat on the floor with Bobby while Annabelle went through to the kitchen. "How have you been?" she shouted, distracting Bobby with his play bricks so he didn't miss his mum too much.

"So-so. You?"

"About the same. Has this little one been giving you the run-around?"

Annabelle appeared in the doorway with two plates piled high with food. "Doesn't he always? Hey, it's a good job you only bought the one portion; there's loads here. It smells delicious." Bobby turned to look at his mother, his interest piqued as the smell wafted into the room. "Don't even think about it, you little rascal. You've been messing me about all day with your meals. This is mummy time and mummy's dinner."

"You get on and eat yours. I'll keep him distracted for a few minutes to give you some peace."

"He's fine. Any bother from him, and I'll put him in the playpen. I'll take him up to bed after we've eaten. I only kept him up so he could see his favourite aunt."

Kayli set a pile of bricks in front of her nephew and said, "See how high you can build it, Bobby. We'll be watching you."

Bobby smiled and clumsily grabbed the first brick, then another, and got a little frustrated when the second brick refused to interlock with the first one.

Kayli grimaced. "Maybe that wasn't the brightest idea I've had all day." She scooped up some chicken and a forkful of noodles and savoured the taste. "This is yummy. I haven't had a Chinese in ages."

"You've lost a lot of weight, Kayli. Looks like you haven't been eating much at all since Mark and Giles left."

"Pot and kettle come to mind. You look as though you've lost a few pounds too."

Chewing on a mouthful of chicken, Annabelle pointed her fork at her son. "Running around after the little man is to blame for that."

Kayli studied Annabelle closely. The usual sparkle in her eyes was missing, her cheeks were pale, and there were large black rings around her eyes. "Are you sleeping okay?"

"A bit hit and miss. Gosh, not sure I can eat any more." Annabelle placed her half-eaten plate of food on the coffee table between them.

"You've hardly eaten anything."

"Nonsense. You eat yours. I'll put Bobby to bed, and then we'll have a natter."

Kayli gave her a concerned look but didn't say anything else while tiny ears were listening in. Annabelle left the room and returned ten minutes later to find Kayli washing the dishes in the kitchen. She didn't have the heart to tell Annabelle that she'd also thrown most of her dinner away, quickly hiding the evidence in the bin beneath the takeaway bag.

Annabelle looked even worse than when she'd left the room. "Do you want a drink?"

"A coffee would be great. I better not drink any alcohol if I have to drive home."

"You could always spend the night in the spare room. It would be lovely to have some company for a change."

"Not that I need much persuading ... go on then, I'll stay. What shall we have? Wine?"

"I think there's a bottle in the fridge. I'll get it." Annabelle walked towards the large stainless-steel American-style fridge but stopped halfway. She tottered a few times on the spot then fell to the floor.

"Annabelle! What's the matter?" Kayli rushed to help Annabelle to her feet.

"Please. The room is spinning. Leave me here for a second."

"I'm going to call the doctor."

"No, don't do that. I'll be fine in a moment."

"Let me get you in the chair. You can't sit on a cold floor." It took all Kayli's strength to lift Annabelle into a chair at the kitchen table.

"I don't know what's wrong with me. One minute, I'm fine. The next, I'm being sick, and it makes me light-headed."

"Lack of sleep and worry can do that to a person."

"I'm not worried about anything."

Kayli tilted her head. "You're not? What about Giles being away? I know both he and Mark are constantly in my thoughts."

"I'm concerned about their safety—of course I am—but I wouldn't necessarily say that I'm worried."

Kayli rushed over to the sink and filled a glass with water. "Here, drink this. We're definitely not having any wine this evening. I'll make you some tea instead."

"Ugh ... can't stand tea."

"Mum always says it cures all illnesses. It'll have to be nice and sweet, though."

"Syrupy tea! That's going to make me puke again."

"How often are you being sick, sweetheart?"

"I don't know. I suppose a couple of times during the day."

"How long has this been going on?"

"Are you interrogating me, DI Bright?"

Kayli shrugged. "I guess I am. Could you be pregnant?"

Annabelle's eyes almost popped out of their sockets, and she gasped. "Shit! The idea never even occurred to me. I just thought I had picked up a slight bug from somewhere."

Kayli reached for her handbag and headed towards the door. "There's only one way to settle this. I'll be right back."

"Kayli, where are you going?"

"Don't move. I'll be two minutes, if that." Kayli ran out the front door and bolted down the street to the pharmacy at the end of Annabelle's road. She immediately located the pregnancy kits on the shelf, paid the shop assistant, and ran all the way home again. She panted rapidly as she let herself in the front door again and stepped into the kitchen. She placed the pharmacy bag on the table in front of Annabelle, who tentatively opened the package.

"Crap! What if I am?"

"There's only one way of finding out. Go pee on the stick—that's an order."

Annabelle stood up without any difficulty and left the kitchen. Kayli heard the toilet door open under the stairs. The minutes passed by as if they were hours.

"Are you all right in there?" Kayli whispered, her ear against the door.

The bolt slid back, and a dazed-looking Annabelle emerged from the tiny room. Her hand shook uncontrollably when she held the tiny test instrument out to Kayli. "It's positive. At least I think that's what the reading says."

"Come and sit down." Kayli took the test from her hand and, supporting Annabelle's arm, led her into the lounge. Once they were both seated on the couch, Kayli studied the test for herself. "Eek, I don't know much about these things, but it looks like a positive result to me. How do you feel?"

"Bewildered, confused, *pregnant*." Annabelle burst into tears and didn't stop for the next five minutes.

Kayli cradled her in her arms and rocked her. "It'll be fine. Bobby will love having a little brother or sister around."

"I suppose so. Crap! What is Giles going to say?"

"We'll find out in a few days. I'm sure he'll be over the moon, lovely. You're worrying about nothing. He adores Bobby."

"I know he does. But what if he thinks I've tricked him into it ... you know, to make sure he stays at home or at least in this country?"

"I know Giles, and that will be the furthest thought from his mind. You're reading too much into this, love. You should be joyful about this. You do want it, don't you?"

"We've never discussed having a second child. I'm not sure how I feel."

"It'll take a while to get used to the idea. After all, you thought you'd picked up a bug."

"Some bug, right?" Annabelle smiled, but it didn't disperse the worry lines around her eyes.

"You aren't handling Giles being away well, are you?"

Annabelle shook her head, and tears filled her eyes. "No, I don't think I am. What about you?"

Kayli sighed and brushed a stray hair behind her ear. "I thought I would be okay, but to be honest with you—and this stays between us—I hate being alone in the house. I miss Mark terribly. We're in a catch-22 situation: if we tell our men how we feel and they give up their jobs, that could put as much strain on our relationships as if we say nothing."

Annabelle nodded. "What is it that is affecting you so much?"

"The danger. The not knowing if they're safe and well. I suppose I'd feel differently if I could speak to Mark every night, but it's been two weeks since they left, and we've heard absolutely nothing from them."

"That's exactly how I feel. Maybe we can talk to them together when they return. You know, voice our concerns openly, supporting each other. What do you think?"

Kayli wiped away a tear from Annabelle's cheek. "I think once Giles finds out he's going to be a father again, he'll jack the job in, but don't quote me on that. I know how his mind works. He'll do anything to make you and Bobby and the new recruit happy."

"I think you're right. If he does reconsider his role, where will that leave Mark? Do you think he'll jack the job in, too?"

"I wouldn't have thought so. He's the security manager, so he has more responsibility than Giles. I could never fathom that one out. Giles was always the higher-ranking officer between them in their army days."

Annabelle nodded. "I must admit, I thought it was strange too. I feel a little better now. I know wine is out of the question, but do you think I could have a cup of coffee instead? Can't stand the taste of tea."

"Of course, I'll make it now." Kayli hugged Annabelle before she stood up. "Congratulations. Mum and Dad are going to be thrilled."

"Let's keep it between us for now. I better make an appointment at the doctor's to get it confirmed before I tell Giles. I'll ring them in the morning."

"I'm delighted that we found out the cause of why you were feeling out of sorts. It's great news all round, hon." Kayli stepped into the kitchen to make two cups of coffee. While the kettle boiled, she stared out the window at the dark sky, wondering what the boys were up to and how Giles would indeed react when he heard the news. Then a selfish thought entered her mind. *What if Giles does give up his job to stay at home with Annabelle and Bobby? Where would that leave Mark?*

She had no idea if either of them was even enjoying their new roles, but she would find that out when the men returned on Friday. A tiny part of her hoped that Mark regretted his decision to accept the job, but where would that leave him if he did? Back at home, slouching around, complaining that no one was willing to take a chance on him and offer him employment? They were between a rock and a hard place. Friday was crunch day for her family. She had no doubts in her mind whatsoever what Giles's plans would entail. However, what Mark's decision would be was lost on her.

"Where's that coffee?" Annabelle called out impatiently from the lounge. "I think you'll find a slice of fruitcake in the breadbin if you fancy a piece."

"Do you want some?"

"Yes, go on then. Cut a slice, and I'll have a nibble on it, see if I can keep it down."

Kayli did as was requested and carried the two mugs of coffee and the slice of cake into the lounge. "Hey, you definitely look more cheerful than when I arrived, even after your mishap in the kitchen."

"It's taken the weight off my mind. I'm not going to get excited until the doctor has confirmed it, though. I hope he can do that before Friday."

"I heard that it's tough getting an appointment nowadays, so tell him it's an emergency."

"Will do. Where's that cake?"

They spent the next few hours reminiscing about the holidays they had shared together as a family before Bobby had come along and about the antics Mark and Giles got up to when they were abroad in Italy and Spain.

Kayli sighed. "What I wouldn't give for a holiday in the sun right now."

"Maybe we can arrange for all of us to go away in the summer next year."

"Umm ... aren't you forgetting something?"

Kayli's eyes widened. She swallowed loudly and grinned. "My God, I've just had the most amazing idea."

"Well, are you going to tell me what that is?" Annabelle asked, amused.

"Mark and I could get married on a paradise island somewhere. On the edge of the beach as the waves gently ripple around our legs."

"That would be *sooo* romantic, Kayli."

She noticed her sister-in-law's smile had altered slightly. "With you and Giles, of course, and Bobby."

Annabelle's smile broadened once more. "How cool." She rubbed her tummy. "Depending on this little one."

"Damn, I forgot about the baby. We can work out your dates once the doctor has confirmed you're pregnant and go from there. I bet it'll be cheaper to get married abroad in the long run too."

"Not sure it'll be cheaper by the time you've factored in the cost of the flights and the hotel, but it'll definitely be more fun and less stress for you both. Do you want me to do some research on the internet for you while you're at work tomorrow, hon? I'd love to help organise it if you'll allow me to."

"Are you kidding me? That would be fabulous, but only if you have the time. Don't feel obligated to do it. I know what a handful Bobby is at times, and you're not feeling your best with the little one who has just announced his or her arrival."

"Nonsense, it'll help take my mind off things." She raised her coffee mug and chinked it against Kayli's. "To you and your exotic wedding. Shall we keep things a secret for now until we've figured out the costs? Wouldn't want to cause Mark a heart attack." Annabelle laughed.

"Well, this new job of his is supposed to be bringing in mega-bucks, so we should be able to afford it. Of course, we'll pay for you guys to come too. You'll just need to find a bit of spending money, that's all."

"Gosh, it's definitely something to look forward to. It's almost eleven. Do you think we should call it a day now?"

"I think so. Although I doubt I'll get much sleep now. I'm too excited."

"You will. You'll be dreaming about your wedding for months to come. I wish Giles and I had just taken off somewhere; our wedding was such a bloody hassle to organise. I think this is an ideal solution, and what's more—you get your honeymoon thrown in at the same time. Do you really want us all there with you on your honeymoon?"

Kayli's cheeks warmed. "Of course! Bloody hell, I'm super excited by the thought now. We should do everything we can to make this happen now the seed has been sown."

"Right, for now, though, we should call it a day. The bed should be already made up. I'll just check on that for you."

"Thanks, Annabelle. This evening has been just what we both needed to put the world to rights. We should do it more often if the boys are going to be away all the time with their jobs."

Annabelle left the couch and bent over to hug Kayli. "It was a welcome surprise and one that I think we should definitely revisit soon. Goodnight, hon."

"I'll just wash up the mugs and be straight up. Goodnight, Annabelle."

After Annabelle left the room, Kayli gathered the mugs and whisked them into the kitchen before she made her way up the stairs to bed. She had no idea if sleep would arrive soon, considering how excited she felt, but she gave it a shot anyway.

CHAPTER FOUR

Adam Finley left the pub at his usual time after his darts match ended. It was his second year of being on the pub team. They were riding high in the league, and he was billed as their star player.

Wearing a satisfied grin, he jumped behind the wheel of his car and set off for home. His wife, Anita, would be waiting for him. He'd already rung ahead and ordered a fish-and-chip takeaway to be delivered by the local chippie, and he started to salivate just thinking about the welcoming smell that would greet him when he walked through the front door.

He was about to turn onto the B4054 when a motorbike cut him up, going at a speed of well over seventy miles an hour. The manoeuvre forced Adam to slam on his brakes. He punched the car horn with the heel of his hand and left it there for several seconds, adding a shake of his fist for good measure when the driver looked over his shoulder and issued him with a V-sign.

"Arsehole. Why don't you have some consideration for other road users? Bloody moron! And they wonder why there are more accidents on the British roads ... is it any wonder, with tossers like that being let loose?" Voicing the sentiment seemed to calm him down. Continuing on his journey, he upped the sound on the stereo and listened to the new eighties' CD he'd purchased only a few weeks ago on a nostalgic whim. He drummed his fingers to the beat of 'Club Tropicana' by Wham! and shook his head. *What a waste, Georgie boy. You were so talented. Of course, your music will live on forever, but it won't be the same without you popping up on our screens now and again.* "Why do so many talented musicians die so young? Prince, Whitney, Michael Jackson, and George, to name but a few. What a bloody waste!"

Adam rounded the corner on the long stretch of road and saw a bike pulled up alongside the barrier. Peering over the steering wheel, he grinned. "That'll teach you, you bastard. I hope you're stuck there for hours until the recovery vehicle comes to rescue you."

As he approached the bike, the driver looked up and started gesturing for him to pull over.

"Fuck off. It's not going to happen, matey. Maybe that will teach you to be more considerate towards fellow drivers next time." He smiled as he drove past then looked in his rear-view mirror to see what the driver's reaction was to being ignored.

The driver turned to look down the road after him, his hands planted firmly on his hips. Adam laughed. He had the feeling the driver was a tad irate. Then the man mounted his bike again and started the engine.

"What the fuck are you playing at? Is there something wrong with your bike or not?" He slowed down to see what happened next.

The driver pulled into the lane behind him.

"Unbelievable! You sneaky little shit. What the heck are you up to?"

Adam sensed he should get out of there as soon as he could. He pressed his foot down on the accelerator, and his estate car lurched forward, slamming his head into the headrest. With one eye on the road, he kept the other trained on the rear-view mirror to gauge what the bike driver's next move would be. He sensed someone was trying to mess with his head.

One minute the motorbike was right behind him, causing his heart to race, and the next, the driver had eased off his throttle and dropped back to within thirty feet again.

Adam was torn whether to pull over and let him pass or continue on his journey. He was only five minutes from home now anyway. The turning he usually took was just up ahead, but Adam was in a quandary whether to take his usual route home or go the long way round instead. That would give him enough time to shake this bastard off his tail. The last thing he wanted to do was lead this lunatic to his front door. *Who knows what would happen then?* He pressed his foot down harder. As he drove past his usual turnoff, a feeling of regret constricted his stomach, but he carried on driving down the long stretch of road, all the time keeping a watchful eye on the aggressive driver behind him.

The bike kept up the momentum of driving close and dropping back, toying with him. The bizarre behaviour was so distracting that Adam's car veered dangerously towards the barrier at one point. He was tempted to pull over and jump out of his car to confront the driver. "People shouldn't be allowed to get away with messing with folks' minds like this. Frigging psycho!"

The bike zoomed forward, got to within inches of Adam's rear bumper, then swerved around his car. As the bike drove past him, Adam pointed to his head and shouted angrily, "You're frigging crazy. I'm going to report you to the police, moron."

Revving his engine, the driver sped away. Adam let out a relieved sigh as he watched the bike's light fade into the distance. His breath caught, though, when the driver slammed on his brakes, angling his vehicle across the middle of Adam's lane.

"What the fuck are you playing at, dickhead? Crap, you're frigging insane."

He indicated and manoeuvred into the other lane. The driver stood there, in the middle of the road, watching Adam drive towards him.

Adam shook his head. "He's a bloody lunatic. The quicker I get past him and out of here, the better."

Twenty feet ahead.

Ten feet ahead.

Adam drove past the driver. He didn't see the bullet as it pierced the glass in his passenger window. Darkness quickly descended.

CHAPTER FIVE

Kayli's mobile rang several times before she tore herself from her dead sleep. She answered it swiftly and quietly, "DI Bright."

"Sorry to wake you, ma'am. It's the control centre. We've got a murder on the B4054, and a message flagged up on the system telling me to alert you immediately."

"Shit! Another accident on the same stretch of road?"

"No accident, ma'am. The driver was shot."

"What? All right, I'll get dressed and get over there now. Do me a favour and ring Dave Chaplin, ask him to attend the scene ASAP." Kayli glanced at the time on her phone. It was only one fifteen. "Damn, look at the goddamn time. He's going to crucify me for this. Give me the exact location, and I'll be there within half an hour."

The officer on control gave her the coordinates and hung up.

Kayli crept along the landing to the bathroom. The door was shut, but she could hear Annabelle being sick inside. She knocked on the door and whispered, "Are you all right, sweetheart?"

"Yeah, my coffee is resurfacing. That's all."

"Poor you. I've just had a call from work. I need to go. There's been a murder. I'll have a quick wash in the downstairs loo."

The toilet flushed, and she heard the lock on the bathroom door slide across. "No, have a shower if you want in here," Annabelle said, her face paler than a snowman's.

"Crap, you look terrible. I'll ring them back, get someone else to attend the scene."

"Don't be daft. I'll be fine. You go. I'm going to collapse into bed anyway."

"As long as you're sure. I'll ring you later to see how you are. Don't forget to make an appointment at the doctor's."

"I won't. Stop worrying about me and get your skates on."

Kayli kissed Annabelle on her cheek. "Ring me if you need me, all right?"

61

"I will. Now go."

Kayli closed the bathroom door and washed quickly after deciding that she didn't have the time to have a shower. She dressed in record time and flew out the front door, closing it quietly behind her. She punched in the postcode the control room officer had given her and set off.

When she arrived at the scene, Dave was there to greet her.

"Sorry for disturbing you, matey. Hope you didn't mind?"

"No bother. I was awake anyway. Suranne was none too pleased, however."

"Damn, send her my apologies when you eventually get home."

"She'll be fine once I explain the situation. This has to be our priority, right?"

"Right. Let's see what we've got. All I've heard is that someone was shot. By the looks of things, another car has gone through the bloody barrier."

"Maybe we should get our guys to patrol this road regularly. This is the second incident to hit this stretch of road in the last twenty-four hours, hardly a coincidence in my book."

Kayli nodded. "I totally agree. We'll get on that in the morning. Can't see the need for it now with this much activity on the road." Kayli and Dave weaved their way through several of the emergency response vehicles to the area that had been cordoned off. She flashed her ID at the officer, who nodded and lifted the tape. "It's not pretty, ma'am."

"Murder rarely is," she replied solemnly.

Dave clung to Kayli's arm as they worked their way cautiously down the steep verge. "I can't believe this has happened again. Why?"

"We won't know that until we find the bastard responsible, gov."

A uniformed officer approached them. "Hello, DI Bright. Thanks for attending."

"No problem, John. What have we got?"

"Looks like a drive-by shooting and the driver ended up down here."

"What? He was shot on the road?"

"That was my initial assessment, ma'am. There's evidence of glass on the road. My take is the driver was dead before he hit the barrier."

"Any witnesses corroborating that, John?"

"No one. The SOCO team are here, and the pathologist is on her way. I took the liberty of calling the accident investigation team out too. Hope that was okay, ma'am?"

"That's exactly what I would have done. Thanks, John. We'll just take a look at the vehicle ourselves."

He stood aside. "Be my guest. The fire brigade is about to leave. Not a lot they can do to save the victim now."

"Understandable. Pass on my thanks for attending." Kayli stepped closer to the vehicle. What she saw made her stomach tie itself in knots. Bile rose in her throat when she noted the amount of blood covering the damaged windshield. The car had rolled at some point during its descent but had righted itself where it landed. She peered through the shattered passenger window at the driver. His head was half blown away. She retched and stood away from the car.

"Are you all right?" Dave asked.

"I will be. He won't, though. Shit, I'm hoping he didn't know what hit him and that death was instant. We need to get an ID on him, Dave."

"I'll have a word with the SOCO team." He walked over to a couple of white-suited technicians and returned with an evidence bag. He slipped on the blue gloves the technicians had also supplied him with and opened the bag containing the man's wallet. "Here we go. He's Adam Finley."

"Note his address down. We'll shoot over there after we leave here. Ah, here's Naomi now." She watched the pathologist navigate her way carefully down the embankment and walk towards them.

"Haven't even visited my bed tonight yet. I had a fatal crash to attend five miles away. I was about to pack up and go home when the call came in about this one. Can't believe anyone would deliberately shoot someone on this stretch of road. Nothing should surprise me nowadays, but it still does."

"I know what you mean. It's a gruesome one, Naomi. The guy never stood a chance. We've got his ID, he lives a few roads away. I'd say he was a regular user of the road, which could mean he was targeted for a reason. On the other hand, he might have been in the wrong place at the wrong time. No witnesses, which will make our task a lot harder. Still, that's my problem, not yours."

"I'll do my best to do the PM tomorrow—what am I saying? Today—and get the report back to you ASAP. Do you think this one is connected to the other crime?"

Kayli shrugged. "In my mind, it's too much of a coincidence. We better keep an open mind on it for now, though, right?"

"As always, until something significant turns up. I better get on. I'll be in touch soon."

Kayli stepped aside to allow Naomi access to the vehicle. "There's nothing much we can do here, Dave. We should go and inform the family."

"I agree. Maybe we can come back when it's daylight to have a better look?"

"Done deal. It's hard to see things clearly as it stands. You might need to give me a shove up the hill again."

"So what's new? I'm always lending you a hand to rise up in the world."

"Funny, even for this time in the morning."

They jumped in their respective vehicles and drove to Finley's address. Kayli was surprised to see a light on in the front room of the house. She met up with Dave outside the property and said, "Looks like someone was waiting up for Adam to arrive home."

"Looks that way to me. God, I hate this part of the bloody job." Dave sighed.

"You're not alone there."

On heavy legs, they walked up the small path to the white rendered semi-detached house. Dave rang the bell while Kayli inhaled and exhaled a few times to prepare herself.

The door swung open within seconds. A woman in her thirties was standing in the doorway, fully clothed, with mascara-streaked cheeks. "Yes?"

"Mrs. Finley? I'm DI Kayli Bright, and this is my partner, DS Dave Chaplin. Would it be possible for us to come in and speak with you for a moment?" Kayli held up her ID at the same time.

The woman leaned forward to get a closer look. "It's Adam, isn't it?"

Kayli nodded.

The woman stepped behind the door to allow them access into the house. Kayli and Dave stood awkwardly in the hallway until she closed the door and showed them into the lounge. The remains of a fish-and-chip takeaway lay on the table. Mumbling an apology, Mrs. Finley quickly wrapped up the parcel then rushed out of the room. She returned seconds later and gestured for them both to take a seat. Once seated, she asked, "Is he in hospital?"

"I'm sorry. Unfortunately, Mrs. Finley, it is with regret that I have to tell you Adam was involved in an incident this evening."

"It's Anita. What sort of incident? Is he okay? I was expecting him home hours ago."

Kayli swallowed the lump that had filled her throat and shook her head. "No, your husband died at the scene."

Her eyes widened in disbelief. "He what? No. He couldn't have. You've made a terrible mistake. I only spoke to him a few hours ago. This can't be happening. Not to us."

Kayli let out a shuddering breath. "I'm so sorry for your loss. We received the call an hour ago to say that there had been a possible drive-by shooting. When we arrived at the scene, Adam had already passed away."

Anita's hand slapped against her right cheek. "He was *shot*? How? Why? My God! Who on earth would do such a thing?"

"Yes, he was shot. There was no way he would have survived his wounds."

"What does that mean?"

"Just that if it's any consolation, Adam's death would have been instantaneous."

"Oh right. And you think that news should reassure me? I'm sorry to snap, but you've just told me my husband has been killed and ..." She broke down and sobbed.

Kayli left her seat to comfort the woman, who flinched when Kayli touched her hand. She held back, unsure how to proceed. "Maybe I should call someone to be with you?"

"I don't have any family here if that's what you're asking. It was just me and Adam. My family are all back in Scotland. They're miles away."

"I'm sorry. Perhaps there is a friend I can ring?"

"No one at this time of the morning. Have you caught the person?"

"Not yet. But we will do. It's only a matter of time."

"A matter of time? Are you just going to sit around and wait for this person to strike again?" Anita covered her face with her hands, uttering a barely audible apology.

"We'll get the investigation underway immediately. There are cameras on that stretch of road, which will aid us. Rest assured that we won't stop until we find the culprit and bring them to justice. I have to ask if Adam had any enemies?"

"But you said this was a drive-by shooting. I'm confused. Are you now telling me that you think someone deliberately set out to kill him?"

"Not necessarily, but we need to cover all the angles from the outset. Are you sure Adam hasn't fallen out with anyone at work, for instance?"

"No, never. Adam was a very easy-going kind of man, got on with everyone. Jesus, I can't believe I'm never going to see him again. We've been married for ten years, just celebrated our anniversary last week. We're due to fly out to Mauritius in a couple of weeks ..." Fresh tears began to cascade down her cheeks.

Kayli placed a hand over Anita's, and this time, the woman accepted the comforting gesture. "I'm so sorry." She looked over at Dave for help.

He shrugged and grimaced.

"How do people get hold of these guns? Is it even legal in the UK to carry one?"

"No, it's not. They generally get them through the underground, obtain them illegally. Our hands are tied."

"You must know the people bringing these weapons to our streets. What are you lot doing about it?" Anita demanded angrily.

Kayli looked at the woman. She was used to people striking out at the police when a loved one had died. Anita was right, she and her colleagues should be doing more to combat the illegal arms business that was rife in the UK. However, with the cuts every force was experiencing, it was a devil of a job keeping up with all the crimes committed on the streets, let alone all the dodgy dealings in weapons taking place in alleyways and in remote areas. "We try our hardest. It's not easy, as you can imagine."

"No, I can't imagine. Every single job I know has advantages and disadvantages, but we still have to deal with them properly."

"I know. Forgive me, I'm not trying to make excuses. It is what it is. I could go on for hours discussing the cuts the government has made, but it would be pointless."

Anita nodded her understanding. "I'm sorry, that was unfair and uncalled for. I have to vent my anger on someone. The love of my life has just been snatched away from me, so someone has to take the brunt of my anger."

"Don't worry, we're used to it. Are you sure I can't ring a friend to be with you?"

"Not at this time of the morning. It wouldn't be fair on them. I'm a strong woman, Inspector. I'll survive."

"I have no doubts about that, but I'd feel better if you had some company after we left."

"Why? Do you think I'm going to top myself?"

Kayli smiled and patted Anita's hand. "The thought never crossed my mind. You shouldn't be alone right now. We're going to have to leave soon, to get on with the investigation, but I'd rather not do that until I know someone is keeping you company."

Anita threw her hands up in the air out of frustration and reached for her handbag sitting at her feet, tucked alongside the couch. "Okay, you win. I'll ring my dear friend, Mandy. She's going to annihilate me for waking her at this ungodly hour."

"I'm sure in the circumstances, she won't mind."

Anita unlocked her phone and scrolled through her contacts, then she hit a button and waited. "Mandy, it's me. Sorry to wake you ..." She didn't get any farther before the situation overwhelmed her.

Kayli gently removed the phone from her hand. "Hello, Mandy, this is DI Bright of the Avon and Somerset Constabulary."

"What? Is something wrong with Anita? Is she all right? Put her back on the phone this instant."

"Anita has rung you to ask if you could possibly come over and sit with her for a while. We appreciate it's very early, but she's just received some bad news and could do with a good friend right now."

"What kind of bad news? Please tell me."

"Her husband was involved in an incident this evening and unfortunately is no longer with us."

"What?" the woman screeched, almost bursting Kayli's eardrum.

"Is it possible for you to come over? Do you need me to arrange for you to be picked up?"

"Let me get dressed. Of course I'll come over. I'll be fifteen minutes, at the most. I can drive myself. Oh my God, this is just awful. Poor Anita."

"Drive carefully. We'll stay here until you arrive."

"On my way now."

Kayli handed the phone back to Anita once Mandy had ended the call at her end. "She's on her way. She didn't seem to mind that we'd rung, if that reassures you, Anita. Can I make you a drink?"

Anita nodded and swiped at the tears on her cheeks. "Thank you, maybe a strong black coffee would help. Make one for yourselves too, while you're at it. There should be enough milk in the fridge."

"We're all right. We can get a cup when we go back to the station. I won't be a second."

Kayli smiled tautly at Dave as she passed him. He looked uneasy, as if being forced to sit with the distraught woman was far outside his comfort zone. Kayli realised it probably was, as he always left that type of thing to her to deal with.

She welcomed the time it took to wait for the kettle to boil in the kitchen. It gave her a chance to gather her thoughts. Kayli was desperate to get back to the station and get on with things. There was no way she would be able to go back home after leaving here. She was hoping that Dave would feel the same way, but that was entirely up to him.

A few minutes later, the kettle had boiled, and Kayli deposited the mug of black coffee on the table beside Anita, who was still wiping her eyes as new tears replaced the old ones constantly. "Here you go. I hope it's not too strong for you."

Anita smiled. "Thank you. Do you think I should ring my family? Adam's mother is pretty frail after having a hip operation, and his father has a dodgy ticker. But they'll hate me for not being the one to tell them."

"Does Adam have any siblings? Perhaps it would be better if *they* broke the news to his parents."

"He has a brother. I haven't spoken to him in years, though, and wouldn't know where to begin. Would you mind ringing him?"

"Of course not. If you get the number for me."

Anita scrolled through her phone again, pressed another contact's number, then passed the phone to Kayli. "Hello, is this Brian Finley?"

"What is this? Who is this? Do you realise what time it is?" he snapped, sounding groggy with sleep.

"I'm sorry to call at an inappropriate time, sir, but it is urgent. I'm DI Kayli Bright calling from Bristol."

"Bristol? What do you want, Inspector?"

"I have some unfortunate news for you, sir. I'm with your sister-in-law, Anita, and she asked me to call you."

"Anita? Why are you there? Have they had a break-in or something?"

"No. It is with regret that I have to inform you that your brother, Adam, was killed in an incident this evening."

The doorbell rang, and Dave left the room to answer it. A woman barged into the lounge moments later and hugged Anita. Both women began to sob, making it difficult for Kayli to hear what Brian was saying. She walked into the kitchen to continue her conversation. "Sorry about that. Anita's friend has just arrived to be with her."

There was silence on the other end of the phone.

"Sir? Brian, are you still there?"

A quiet voice replied, "I'm here. He's dead? How? What kind of incident?"

"Adam was shot. A callous incident."

"Jesus! Do you have the person in custody, Inspector? I'm a solicitor."

"No, not yet. We're hoping to rectify that soon. I'm sorry for your loss. As you can imagine, Anita is beside herself. She wanted Adam's parents to know as soon as possible but didn't want to ring them herself."

"I'll go round there. It's not the type of news they should hear over the phone."

Kayli felt he was chastising her. "I'm sorry. There was no other way I could have told you, what with you being several hundred miles away."

"I wasn't having a go at you, Inspector. I'm grateful that Anita thought to let me know instead of ringing my parents. Neither of them is in the best of health."

"That's why Anita asked me to ring you."

"How was Adam shot?"

"It was a heinous crime, a drive-by shooting. Now that Anita's friend has arrived to be with her, we're going to head back to the station to make a start with our enquiries."

"When did the incident take place?"

"Around eleven this evening. I got the call as I'm investigating another incident that occurred on the same stretch of road, and I attended the scene immediately."

"Another shooting?"

"No. A suspicious death. The control centre saw a loose link and rang me."

"I see. Well, thank you for beginning the investigation straight away. My family and I appreciate that. I'll try and get down there within the next day or so. I'll need to reschedule some clients in order to do that."

"We can meet up if you need to see me. I want to assure you that my team and I will be working around the clock to get the person who did this."

"That's good to hear. Again, thank you for calling. I'll go round and see my parents first thing in the morning. I know Anita is finding it tough. Will you send her my condolences?"

"I will. I'm sorry for your loss. I have your number. I'll keep you informed of our progress."

"I'd appreciate that. Thank you, Inspector. Good luck."

Kayli returned to the lounge to find the two friends hugging each other still and Dave shifting on the spot awkwardly. "Sorry to interrupt. Brian sends his condolences. He's going to visit his parents in the morning and make his way down here in the next few days."

Anita and Mandy separated and dried their eyes.

"Thank you for ringing him," Anita said. "Was he as shocked as I am?"

"Yes. Look, I hate to share the bad news and run, but the sooner we get on with the investigation, the more likely it is we will apprehend the person responsible. Are you sure you're going to be okay?"

Anita sighed and nodded. "Yes, Mandy is here now. Thank you for all you've done so far."

"My pleasure. Here's my card. I'll keep you up-to-date on things as we go when at all possible. The pathologist will ring you shortly, I should imagine."

"Thank you. Will I have to identify my husband?"

"I think his ID has already confirmed who he is, but most family members like to say farewell to their loved ones at the earliest convenience."

"I'd like that. Thank you."

Kayli shook Anita's hand. "I'll be in touch. Take care." She smiled at Mandy. "Thank you for coming over at such short notice, Mandy."

"No problem. I couldn't let Anita down."

Dave and Kayli left the house, and before she got in the car, she asked Dave, "Do you want to go home or carry on working?"

Dave shrugged. "I'm wide awake now. Might as well carry on with our day. Maybe we can knock off early?"

"That was my thought exactly. Of course, we'll have to see how the case progresses first, so no promises."

"Work always comes first with you, doesn't it?"

Kayli opened the car door. "Goes with the territory of being an inspector, I guess."

"Yeah, thought you might say that. I'll see you back at the station."

Dave made his way back to his own car. Kayli set off without waiting for her partner to follow her, eager to get on with things and desperate for her first coffee of the morning.

CHAPTER SIX

By the time the rest of the staff arrived at nine o'clock, Kayli felt as if she and Dave had already put in a full shift. It was going to be an exceptionally long day. Kayli filled the rest of the team in about the incident they had been working on since one o'clock that morning.

Dave had organised the CCTV footage from the cameras on the B4054 to be sent over first thing. When the discs arrived, Kayli tasked Graeme with trawling through them again. It really didn't take him too long to locate Adam's car being followed by a motorbike.

Leaning over Graeme's shoulder to look at the footage, Kayli announced, "Okay, it seems odd that Carmen mentioned a bike, and now this ... I'm willing to stick my neck out and say the two crimes should be connected. We've got nothing else to go on right now, anyway. The question is whether the two victims are connected, or if they were two people in the wrong place at the wrong time."

"Do you think we should ask Carmen's boyfriend if he knew Adam?" Dave asked.

"Yep, there are a few people we need to get out there to see. One thing I forgot to ask Anita in the early hours of this morning was where Adam was playing darts."

"You're thinking it was at the Jolly Roger? The same place Carmen and her mates were drinking the other night?"

Kayli nodded. "Maybe *that's* the link, rather than the victims. I'm just throwing it out there at this early stage. I'll give Anita a ring in an hour or so to find out. Sod it, we need to know now." She walked into her office to place the call. The phone was answered within two rings. "Hi, Anita?"

"No, this is Mandy. Who is this?"

"Hi, Mandy. This is DI Bright. We met earlier this morning. Is Anita around?"

"I ordered her to get some sleep, Inspector. I'd rather not disturb her if that's okay?"

"Of course. Maybe you can answer the question I have."

"I'll do my best."

"Adam was out last night, playing darts at a pub. Any idea which pub that would be?"

"You're in luck, yes. It's the Jolly Roger in Sea Mills."

"You're a star. Thank you, Mandy. How is Anita?"

"A mess. She was strong when you were here, but as soon as you left, she crumbled. Around six this morning, I told her to try and get some rest. I haven't heard her walking around up there for a while, so she must have gone to sleep."

"Damn, I hope my call hasn't woken her. Send her my best wishes and reassurance that we're doing our best to find the culprit now."

"I'm sure she slept through the phone ringing. I'll pass on your message."

"Thank you for taking care of her too, Mandy. You're a good friend."

"I like to think so. Goodbye, Inspector."

Kayli hung up and began jotting down a plan of action before tiredness interrupted her day and forced her into taking the wrong direction. She left her mail unattended, something she never did, and rejoined her team. "Bingo, guys. Adam was at the Jolly Roger, his regular pub, last night."

"I take it we're going to take a trip out there then?" Dave asked.

"Yep, first I want to go to Carmen's place of work. See if there's anything we should be looking at on that front. The more questions we ask, the easier things will be for us in the long run, right?"

"I'm with you on that one. Do you want me to drive?"

"That'd be great, Dave. I can note down the questions I want to ask on the way. Not sure about you, but my mind feels like it's on go-slow already because of lack of sleep. I dread to think what I'm going to feel like come six this evening."

"I'm with you on that one. It's best if we keep ourselves occupied. I think I have a few matchsticks in my drawer in case we need them later."

Kayli laughed. "It might come to that. Graeme, can you try and get a better image of the bike for me? Just so we have it to hand. I might call a press conference in the next day or two."

"I'll see what I can do, boss. I tried to get a good look at the number plate, but it was obscured by mud."

"Do your best. When you can, maybe you can send a copy to my phone? We can ask around at the pub, see if anyone recognises it."

"Good thinking. I'll get onto it now, boss."

"Donna, I want you to contact the control centre. We need to get a patrol keeping a constant eye on the B4054. The driver seems to enjoy wreaking havoc on that stretch of road in particular. I don't want us to be blasé about this."

"I agree. I'll do it now."

"We have a number of stops to make. I'm on the end of the phone if anything else crops up while we're out, guys. See you both later."

~ ~ ~

Twenty minutes later, they pulled up outside the building society where Carmen Drinkwater worked. Kayli showed the girl standing at the reception area her ID and introduced herself. "I'd like to speak to the manager please on an urgent matter."

"Of course, I'll see if he's free. Take a seat," the brunette said, wearing a wary smile. She walked across the tiled floor to the office at the rear. After knocking, she entered the room and reappeared a few seconds later. "Mr. Boyd will see you now. If you'd like to follow me."

They entered the room to find a tall gentleman in his early forties standing in front of his desk, straightening his tie. "Hello, I'm the manager, Mike Boyd. How can I help?"

Kayli slipped her hand into his and introduced herself and Dave before the three of them sat down. "It is with regret, Mr. Boyd, that I have to inform you that Carmen Drinkwater was involved in an accident the night before last in which she lost her life."

Mr. Boyd bounced forward to sit upright in his chair, clearly surprised to hear the shocking news. "What? She's dead? I don't believe it."

"It's true. I'm sorry. I know she's recently achieved a promotion. It's very sad that her life should end when things are going well for her."

"It's just terrible. Unthinkable this should happen to Carmen. She had so much going for her. A great prospect for the future. I believe she would have become a branch manager in the near future had she not ..." His hand covered his face. "I don't know what to say. I'm stunned by this unwanted news."

"It is hard to take in. I'm sorry. Did she have any enemies at work? Had she fallen out with anyone recently?"

His brow wrinkled into a puzzled frown. "I don't understand ... you said she died in an accident. Why are you asking such questions if that was the case?"

"There are accidents and accidents, Mr. Boyd. Some accidents force us into making other enquiries. If you could answer the question ...?"

He shook his head. "No. My staff all get along well. They're always supportive of each other. Crikey, they're going to be devastated by this news."

"Was she especially close to anyone in particular? Maybe we can have a chat with the staff? Would that be possible?"

Mr. Boyd ran a hand over his face. "Yes, she was close to Angela Silverton. She's going to be stunned when she learns of Carmen's death."

Kayli nodded her understanding. "Is there some place we can interview all the staff?"

"Yes, there's a small staffroom at the rear. I can arrange that for you now. I'm at a loss what to say about this. Can I ask how she died?"

She looked him in the eye and said, "A car accident. That's all I'm prepared to say at this point, until we get the pathologist's report back. Thank you. Before we speak to the other members of staff, are you sure nothing comes to mind about any arguments or ill feelings that you've sensed recently?"

"No, I can assure you, there's nothing that has come to my attention. I run a happy ship, and if I discovered anything of that ilk going on, then I would summon the two staff members to thrash things out. No such thing has occurred. You have my word on that, Inspector."

"Okay, that's good to know. If we could interview the staff now? Only we have a few places we need to visit today, and time is of the essence at the start of every investigation."

Mr. Boyd left his chair and walked out of the room. He returned a few moments later and remained in the doorway. "I've arranged for the staff to see you one at a time in the staffroom. Angela will be the first person you see. I haven't told them the nature of your presence. Be gentle with them, Inspector."

"No worries on that front, Mr. Boyd. Thank you for being so accommodating."

He showed them through to the room where the staff enjoyed their breaks. It was a square room that had a kitchenette area and a table with four chairs around it. A window overlooked the staff car park at the rear of the property. Mr. Boyd left them, and a few moments later, a young woman with her blonde hair tied up in a ponytail entered the room.

"Hello. Mr. Boyd asked me to come and see you. I'm Angela Silverton."

Kayli smiled and gestured for the woman to take a seat at the table with her and Dave. "Thank you for seeing us. Our visit here today is primarily to break some bad news, but we'd also like to ask some questions, if that's okay?"

"Bad news?" The young woman gasped. "No, this isn't about Carmen, is it?"

"Why do you ask that, Angela?"

"She didn't turn up for work neither yesterday nor today. I've tried ringing her and received no reply to either my calls or the dozens of texts I've sent. I'm worried about her."

Kayli sighed. "Yes, this is regarding your friend, Carmen. Unfortunately, she was involved in an accident the night before last. She didn't survive."

Tears ran down the woman's heavily made-up face. "I don't believe it! You're telling me that she's dead?"

"I'm afraid so. If it's any consolation, we think she was unconscious for quite a while after the collision."

"It's kind of a relief to know that. My God, I can't believe it. Sorry for repeating myself. Bloody hell, she had so much to live for what with her promotion."

"It's very sad. As you were close to her, maybe you can tell us what her relationship was like with her boyfriend, Lincoln?"

"I don't understand. Why would you want to know that?"

"We're simply dotting all the Is, if you like."

"They were happy enough. They'd have to be if they were talking about getting married, right?"

"I suppose so. No arguments that you can think of?"

She shrugged. "Crikey, everyone has those. Why should they be any different? They always worked around them, though."

"Did you know she was pregnant at the time of her death?"

Angela's hand covered her mouth, and she shook her head.

"I know it's very upsetting for you, but please, can you think back to any recent conversations you've had with Carmen, regarding anyone she might have had a slight contretemps with, perhaps?"

"How awful ... now two lives have been lost. No, I really can't think of anything that might help you. We were close, but we didn't burden each other with our personal lives much. I suppose we saw our time here at work as a release from all the pressures going on at home."

Finding the woman's statement intriguing, Kayli pressed harder, or as hard as she could under the circumstances. "From your point of view or from hers?"

"Both, I suppose. I'm in a dubious relationship, shall we say?"

"Care to enlighten us further?"

Angela sighed, and her gaze dropped down to the pile of magazines sitting in the middle of the table. "No. Let's just say my fella and I are going through a rough time of our own at present."

"I see. Was Carmen aware of this?"

"No. Although I think she suspected all wasn't well at home. She made a point of never sticking her nose in where it wasn't wanted."

"I see. She was indeed a good friend then. There to talk to if you need her but one that knew there were also boundaries between friends."

"That's exactly how we saw things, Inspector. She was a very special lady. We're all going to miss her around here. That's for sure."

Kayli nodded. "Are there any male members of staff here?"

"Only the manager and the mortgage manager, her immediate boss."

"And how did they get on with Carmen?"

"Very well. They appreciated her aptitude for mortgages, hence why Mr. Boyd promoted her so quickly."

"Quickly? You mean ahead of others at the branch?"

"Yes. I can see where you're going with this, and you couldn't be further from the truth. We were all ecstatic for Carmen when she went for the job. No one thought badly of her jumping ahead of them. We support each other's careers at this branch, no backbiting or bitchiness. Everyone has the chance to go for promotion when the timing is right for them. Some people prefer to put their families first and to avoid any extra pressure that this type of promotion throws at them. Carmen had a lot of surplus studying to do in that respect once she left here at night, but with Lincoln working opposite shifts to her, she was craving something to fill her evenings."

"So there could have been some animosity between Carmen and her boyfriend. Is that what you're saying?"

"I suppose I am in a roundabout way. She always had her head in her studies during her lunch hour, so I guess she'd be the same at home on her days off and in the evenings. However, Lincoln and Carmen didn't really see much of each other. Maybe I'm talking bullshit there." She grimaced, as if to apologise for her bad language.

"We need to question Lincoln, so we'll see what he has to say about that. Did Carmen ever mention if she'd had a problem with a customer perhaps? Or maybe a neighbour who was pestering her?"

"Nothing that I can think of. Again, I don't see why you're asking these questions if she was involved in an accident."

"It's just something we do with every accident," Kayli lied, determined to keep her suspicions under wraps for the moment. "Is there anything else you can think of that might be of interest to us?"

"No, nothing. Maybe something will come to mind once my head is a little clearer. I'm a bit overwhelmed by the news, if I'm honest."

"Sorry. It's always sad when we hear about someone losing their life together with their unborn child."

"You're not wrong there, especially when Carmen had so much to live for. Did she know about the baby?"

"Yes, she was aware. Apparently, she wanted to keep it quiet until after her twelve-week scan. Her boyfriend was unaware of the baby, however."

"Poor Lincoln. How dreadful for him. How will he cope?"

"I'm sure he'll be fine. Time is a great healer."

"Can I get back to work now?"

"Yes, would you mind sending the next person in? Thank you for all your help, and I'm sorry for your loss."

"Thank you."

When Angela left the room, Dave said, "Something isn't sitting right with this boyfriend of hers. Don't ask me to pinpoint what it is, but there's something that's prodding me to dig deeper on him."

"You think? I'm not so sure. Donna carried out a full check on him and came up with zilch. It's not as if Angela said Lincoln and Carmen argued a lot. By all accounts, they rarely saw each other."

"I know, but ..." His voice drifted off when another young woman knocked on the door and entered the room.

They spent the next few hours questioning all the staff, but frustratingly for Kayli, they all had nothing but kind words to say about Carmen. Before leaving the premises, Kayli and Dave sought out the manager again to thank him for his cooperation.

"Where are we going now?" Dave asked once they were strapped into the car.

"Let me check if Graeme has sent that image to my phone yet." She opened her messages app to find it empty, then she rang the station. "Graeme? I haven't received the image of the bike yet. Is there a reason for that?"

"Sending it through now, boss. Sorry for the delay. I wanted to send you the best image I could find. I think this one will suffice."

"Great. We're heading over to the Jolly Roger now. We should be back soon."

"Good luck."

Dave drove them to the pub on the outskirts of Sea Mills. The exterior of the pub was in dire need of a good paint, but inside, it felt super cosy. The pub was somewhere she wouldn't mind visiting once Mark arrived home from his manoeuvres. She made a mental note to ring Annabelle once she got back to the station to see if she'd kept to her word to make an appointment with the doctor.

As Kayli approached the bar, a young man smiled and asked, "How are you doing, folks? What can I get you to drink?"

Tempted to have a glass of wine, partaking in one likely meant she would fall asleep at her desk once she got back to the station. She produced her warrant card and said quietly, so the other customers couldn't overhear, "Is the manager around?"

The man leaned toward her and said, "You're speaking to him. Phil Drake."

Kayli sniggered. "Sorry. Crikey, you don't look old enough to be drinking in a pub, let alone running one."

"You wouldn't be the first to make that assumption. Believe it or not, I'm actually twenty-nine."

"Really? Wow, you must have good genes in that case, Phil."

"I have. How can I help you, Inspector?"

"Can we speak to you privately?" Kayli asked, sensing a few of the locals turning their way.

"You'll have to wait ten minutes until my barmaid arrives. She just rang to say that she's held up in traffic on the B-road, because of some incident or other."

"No problem. We'll take a seat over there, if that's okay?"

"Sure. Can I get you a drink?"

"I'll have a pi ... maybe a coffee would be better," Dave said.

Amused, Kayli nodded. "Two coffees would be lovely. Thank you."

Phil poured the two coffees and refused payment when Kayli handed him a ten-pound note. "On the house. I'll be with you shortly."

Kayli led the way through the small gathering of customers, some more intrigued than others, to a table close to the window. "This seems a nice place. Have you been here before, Dave?"

"No, never. I wonder what their food is like."

"Excellent," the old man on the next table replied.

"Is that so? Then we'll definitely have to come out here and sample it for ourselves soon, in that case." Kayli smiled at the gentleman, who tipped his flat cap at her. "I need to ring my sister-in-law while I've got five minutes." She picked her mobile up from the table and punched a button. "Hello you. How are you feeling this morning?"

"As sick as the proverbial dog. How are you? I was expecting you to come back after you'd attended the scene."

"Sorry. Dave and I decided it wouldn't be worth it by the time we'd got to the scene and visited the victim's next of kin. Have you made the appointment yet?"

"Yes, they squeezed me in first thing. I should know the results by the end of the day, but the doctor said the over-the-counter pregnancy tests nowadays are pretty accurate."

"I guess congratulations are in order then."

"If it wasn't for this damn morning sickness, I think I'd be over the moon ... at least, I think that's what's holding me back."

"I'm sure it is. Did he give you anything for the sickness?"

"No. He said there was something available on the market, but his advice has always been to put up with it."

"Charming, well, he's not the one bloody suffering. Do you want me to drop by this evening?"

"That would be lovely. I'll make us something nice for dinner."

"Don't do anything special for my sake. Have a restful day instead. Gotta fly, see you later."

"Take care, Kayli. Thanks for ringing."

Kayli smiled as Phil walked towards them, putting paid to Dave's inquisitiveness to find out what the conversation had involved.

"All right to talk here, or do you want to come through to the back?"

"Would you mind?" Kayli stood and picked up her mug of coffee to take with her. She and Dave followed the young manager through the bar, under the watchful gaze of the customers and the barmaid who'd just begun her shift.

He guided them through to a small office that looked tired and in need of decoration. "Let me find a couple of chairs. I'll be right back." He left the office and returned carrying two plastic chairs that had also seen better days. "Here you go. Now, what can I do for you? I don't get many visits from the police. I hope no one has felt the need to complain about us?"

Kayli smiled and placed her mug on the edge of his desk. "No, it's nothing like that. I suspect the reason your barmaid was held up this morning is because of an incident that took place in the early hours on the B4054."

"I see. But I'm still confused. What does that have to do with me?"

"A man was shot last night, and when we visited his wife to share the sad news, she told us that her husband was at a darts match at this establishment just before the incident occurred."

Phil scratched the light beard covering his chin. "He was? Does this man have a name?"

"Adam Finley."

Phil's eyes widened, and his hand settled on his cheek. "My God, Adam was shot? I find this incredible, Inspector. Who would do such a thing? Was it intentional?"

"Well, we're just beginning our enquiries now, so we have no idea if he was specifically targeted or not. We're hoping that you can shed some light on whether anything out of the ordinary occurred here last night?"

He shook his head in either disbelief or denial; Kayli wasn't really sure. "I can't think of anything. We had a league match last night. Darts. He was crowned our star player at the end of the evening. Crap, you don't think someone from the other team did this? Sour grapes, perhaps?"

"That seems a little over the top to me, but it's definitely something we're going to have to look into. We'll need the details of everyone involved in the darts match, so we can question them."

"Blimey, that's a little out of my realms, I'm afraid, Inspector. I can give you the name of the other pub involved. You'll need to get the players' details off them, though."

"Thanks, that'll be great. Can you give me the details of the players in your team?"

"A few of them, I can. Hold on. I might not have their addresses, but I should have their phone numbers, if that will help?"

"It will be a great help. My team can work their way through the list when we get back to the station. How many members are there in a team?"

"Ten."

Kayli's heart sank at the prospect of questioning twenty people. She would definitely need to share the workload with her team on that task. "Do you happen to know if any of the players—or customers, come to that—ride a motorbike?"

He thought about the question for a second or two before he shook his head. "Not that I know of. Saying that, I was busy inside the pub last night and don't think I ventured outside at all. We put on a good spread for the players. I was busy overseeing the catering side of things mainly."

"I see. I don't suppose you have CCTV on the premises?"

He bit his lip, and the colour rose in his cheeks. "I do. But it's knackered. I need to replace the whole system, and to be honest with you, funds are super tight right now. I'll get around to changing it soon, I hope. I know that doesn't help you much."

"These things happen. For your sake, you should have a system up and running at all times."

He shrugged. "I know. I just thought having the cameras outside would be as much as a deterrent than anything. I'll start putting some money aside to address the problem. I'm sure you're aware how many pubs are struggling to keep their heads above water, though. These are trying times for all of us, but enough of my woes. How else can I help?"

"I'm aware how many pubs are being forced to close down. It's not good. You seem to be busy enough. Let's hope that continues to be the case so you can afford to get your security system up and running again soon. Can you tell me how well you knew Adam? Was he a frequent visitor beyond the darts team?"

"Yes, I've known Adam for a few years, since I took over running this place. He was one of the first people to shake hands and congratulate me, in fact. We've been firm friends ever since."

"Firm friends as in that he told you what was going on in his life perhaps?"

"No, only at the pub. He came here for a quiet drink quite often. Occasionally, he would bring Anita, and they'd have a meal in the restaurant. But this was definitely his local. If you're asking if he had any trouble with the other punters, then I'd have to say no, never. I never got the impression that he was any kind of troublemaker."

"That's exactly the type of thing I wanted to hear. Which is why we're going along the lines that he was probably simply targeted for being on that road at the wrong time."

"Seriously? Do people truly kill other people just because they can?"

"You'd be surprised. We have spotted a motorbike on CCTV footage, however. Are you sure you can't think of anyone in the area who owns a motorbike?"

"No. It wouldn't even help if you told me the make. Nothing is coming to mind."

"That's okay. What about your barmaid? Is she likely to know?"

"We can ask. She was also on duty last night." He sighed as if his friend's death had just struck him. "Poor Adam and poor Anita. Is she all right?"

"She has a friend with her at present. Okay, if you can't think of anything else that would be of help, then we better get off. Would you mind if we had a brief chat with your barmaid on the way out?"

"Be my guest. I'll go fetch her, if you like?"

"Thanks, it shouldn't take long."

He left the room, and a few moments later, the young redhead who had turned up for work late knocked on the door and entered the room. "The boss said you wanted to see me?"

"Come in. What's your name?"

"Liz. Liz Dodds."

"Hi, Liz. I just need to ask a few quick questions about your shift last night. Take a seat."

The young woman sat in the seat recently vacated by her manager and rested her elbows on the table. "Okay. What do you want to know?"

"Do you know Adam Finley?"

"I know a player on the darts team called Adam. Not sure what his surname is, though."

"That's the one. Last night, did you see him get into an altercation with anyone?"

"Altercation? No. Everyone had a good time here last night. Not that we get much bother in the pub anyway. My boyfriend wouldn't allow me to work here if it was a rowdy pub like that."

"Okay, that's good to know. Did you go outside during your shift at all?"

"Yes, I'm a smoker. I went outside a few times during the night. Why?"

"Did you notice a motorbike in the car park at all?"

She contemplated the question for a moment before she shook her head. "No, I can't say I noticed one. Not that I was looking for one. Sorry to be so vague. I was only out there for five minutes at a time."

"No problem."

"Sorry, but is Adam in any kind of trouble?"

Kayli had assumed that Phil would have told her why they were there when he'd swapped places with her. "No. Unfortunately, he was killed in an incident up the road last night."

"Jesus, really? My God. I've never known anyone who'd died before. Sorry, that was a stupid statement ... oh no, his poor wife."

"She's being cared for by a friend. Have you ever known Adam to have an argument with one of the customers at all?"

"No. Definitely not. He wasn't the type. Even when he wiped the floor with the other team last night, they all took it in good spirits. No one fell out with anyone, as it's only a bloody game."

"Thanks for your time. You can go now."

She left the room. Dave and Kayli downed the rest of their coffee and returned to the bar. Phil was in deep conversation with a tall bearded man standing at the bar. Both men turned their way as they walked towards them.

In a hushed voice, Phil introduced the man. "Inspector, this is Paul Moore. I think he has something of interest for you."

"I'm all ears, Mr. Moore. Why don't we talk over there?" Kayli pointed at a seat by the unlit fireplace, away from the other customers.

He sighed heavily before he opened his mouth to speak. "We weren't gossiping, but Phil just told me about poor Adam. Dreadful news to be confronted with, I can tell you."

"It's a very sad case for us to be investigating. What do you know, Mr. Moore?"

"Not sure it's much. I was on my way here after I finished the late shift at the factory and saw Adam driving home last night."

Kayli raised an eyebrow at Dave, who swiftly withdrew his notebook from his pocket. "I see. Where exactly was this?"

"Before the roundabout going on to the B4054, just down the road from here. I used to chat with Adam every now and again. Nice guy, he was."

"I see. Did he acknowledge you at all?"

"Yes, he gave me the thumbs-up. Like he always did."

"Okay, and could you tell if he was being followed at all?" Kayli purposefully didn't mention the motorbike. She didn't want to put the idea in his head.

"Ah, well, Phil said that you were enquiring about a motorbike. There was a Harley-Davidson following Adam last night. Frankly, I thought it was too close to him. I presumed it was about to overtake him."

"That's interesting. I don't suppose you got the registration number? I know it's a long shot."

"No, I'm sorry. I was in too much of a hurry to get here."

"Never mind. We do have the bike on CCTV, but the number plate was obscured, so you probably wouldn't have been able to have seen anything anyway. I just thought I'd ask to be sure. Did you recognise the bike at all? Have you seen it in the area, perhaps?"

His brow furrowed. "You know what, now you've mentioned it, I saw one very similar a few days ago on the same stretch of road. Don't ask me what night it was. One day blurs into the next with me."

"That's very helpful. Have you noticed it at any other times in the area?"

"No. Can't say I have. Sorry."

"That's fine. Anything else you can add, Mr. Moore?"

He shook his head in regret. "Not that I can think of. Will you need me to come down the nick to make a statement?"

"If you wouldn't mind. That would be very helpful. Over the next few days will do."

"I'll pop in later before I go to work. Might as well get it out of the way." He was the first to stand.

"Thank you." Kayli shook his hand to dismiss him.

"Interesting," Dave said as they watched the man walk back to the bar.

"Very. What does it mean, though? That Adam was targeted? Or was the bike simply following him?"

"No idea. Not sure how we're going to find that out without catching the culprit. Hey, one good thing has come out of the interviews."

Kayli inclined her head. "What's that, matey?"

"To me, it looks like the bike belongs to a local. That should narrow it down, now we have the make of the vehicle. The CCTV footage was a little blurry to make out it was a Harley."

"Shit! You've just reminded me. I have the image of the bike on my phone." She rushed over to where Paul Moore was drinking a pint at the bar. Flicking through her phone, she pulled up the image of the bike then angled the screen towards him. "Was this the motorbike, Mr. Moore?"

"That's right. That's the one." His head bobbed excitedly up and down.

Liz pulled Kayli's arm towards her and peered at the tiny screen. She shook her head. "Nope, sorry. Not seen the bike around these parts."

Kayli's last hope was the manager. Liz passed Kayli's phone back to him and held it in front of him while he poured a pint of beer for a customer.

"Sorry, no. I've never seen it around here, either."

"Would you mind if I asked the rest of your customers, Phil?"

"Not at all. Go for it."

Kayli approached the other customers, fourteen of them in total, and every single one of them shook their head. Kayli made her way back to Dave, feeling a little dejected. Or maybe she was more tired than she realised. They *had* been at work for nearly twelve hours already.

As if sensing what she was thinking, Dave rubbed her arm. "Come on, chin up. We should go back to the station."

"You're right. We have all these people to call when we return. Thanks for your help, everyone," Kayli called out before they exited the pub.

During the journey back, Dave coughed to clear his throat. "Tell me to keep my nose out if you want to."

"Go on."

"When you were on the phone to Annabelle, did I pick up that she's not very well?"

Kayli turned to smile at him. "Not sure if some people class pregnancy as an illness or not."

"Whoa! That came out of the blue, didn't it? Does your brother know?"

"No. To be honest, Annabelle didn't even suspect she was pregnant. My detective skills came to the fore last night. She looked rough, almost passed out on me. Once she was settled, I ran down the road to the pharmacy to buy a kit. It was a positive result, but she went to the doc's this morning to confirm it. She'll know for sure later on today."

"Bloody hell. That's poor timing, what with Giles working away. Will he still do that? Or give up the job to stay closer to home during the pregnancy?"

"All good questions, Dave. I have no idea what the answers are going to be. I suppose we'll find out soon enough. He and Mark are due home on Friday."

"That must be a relief for you. I know you don't like to moan, but I have sensed that you've missed him while he's been away."

"You're an astute man. You're right, though. What's the point in moaning about it at work?"

"I only have to see the weight you've lost to confirm it."

"Haven't had much of an appetite since he left. Neither has Annabelle. She needs to look after herself more, though, if she does have a bun in the oven."

He tutted and mumbled, "You women sure like to complicate matters."

Kayli dug him in the ribs.

CHAPTER SEVEN

Kayli and Dave arrived back at the station laden down with food for the team. They tucked into their lunch with vigour, especially as Kayli and Dave had foregone their breakfast that morning.

After lunch, they discussed the case at length. "Donna, any luck with tracking down Carmen's ex-boyfriend?"

"I searched the flight schedules, boss, and he definitely hasn't returned to the country since he left."

"Under his name, right? That doesn't mean to say that he hasn't come back under a pseudonym."

"That's a tad Agatha Christie-ish, boss, even for your mind." Dave chortled.

"The truth nevertheless. What other loose ends need tying up?" Kayli threw out to the team, suddenly feeling tired after eating.

"We've got all these names to chase up. You know, the darts teams?" Dave reminded her, clearly more awake than she was.

Kayli sipped her coffee then nodded. "Yes, we should get on to that straight away. Dave, Graeme, and I will do that. Donna, I'd like you to try and find out how many Harley-Davidsons there are in the Bristol area. That'll be the initial search, and then narrow it down to specific areas once that's been established."

"Good idea. I'll get on it now." Donna shuffled forward in her chair and started hitting the keys on her keyboard.

"If you guys start ringing the darts team members, I'll tackle the paperwork I neglected to touch this morning and will catch up with you in an hour or so." She walked into her office and closed the door. After opening the window to allow the afternoon breeze to enter the room, she continued to her desk. As she was halfway through her mundane chores, the phone rang. "Hello, this is DI Bright. How can I help you?"

"Hello, Inspector. I'm sorry to trouble you, but I was wondering if you'd found who was responsible for Carmen's accident yet?"

"Is that you, Jacky?"

"Yes, sorry. I should have said right away."

"No problem. We haven't as yet, because another incident has cropped up. That's not to say that we've pushed Carmen's case aside. We believe there could be a possible link, and this other case has offered us more clues."

"I see. Another accident, you mean?"

"No, this time the victim was shot."

Jacky gasped. "My goodness. I never thought I'd hear of that sort of thing happening in Bristol. I know we've had a drugs problem in the area in the past, but guns?"

"We're hearing more and more cases such as this lately, unfortunately. We're doing our best to crack down on the gun and knife culture, but it's proving to be an impossible task despite the gun amnesties we've had over the past few years."

"Do you know who shot this person?"

"Not yet. But some valuable clues have just come our way that my team is chasing up as we speak. It's only a matter of time before something breaks in these cases. I'm certain of that. How are you holding up, Jacky?"

There was silence on the other end of the line for a few seconds before Jacky sniffled. "One minute, I'm fine, and the next, I'm a mess. I try not to show my emotions in front of the baby, but sometimes, they catch me out. I miss her terribly. We were always at the end of the phone for each other. I doubt my life will ever be the same again, Inspector."

"That's regrettable. I have a brother who I'm exceptionally close to, and if I lost him, I'm sure I'd be feeling the same as you are. Maybe once the funeral has been held and Carmen is laid to rest, things will be different. Don't quote me on that, though, as I've never lost anyone close myself before. Please, try and hang in there."

"I will. Thank you. I just feel so alone."

"What about Lincoln? Has he rung you at all?"

Jacky groaned. "Has he heck. Not a solitary call. Not that I was expecting him to."

"That's strange. I know things were a little tense between you at the hospital, but I thought he would have realised how upset you were and stayed in touch. May I ask who is sorting out the funeral arrangements?"

"That task has landed on my shoulders, not that I'd want it any differently. I don't think men are up to the task of organising things like that, do you?"

Kayli nodded as if Jacky were in the room with her. "I think you have a valid point there. Jacky, is there something you're not telling me about Lincoln? Your reaction to him at the hospital seemed a little—forgive me here if I read the signs the wrong way ... but I felt you were a tad harsh on him. Is there a reason for that, or was it simply because you were upset about Carmen?"

Her question was met with another silence and a large sigh. "I suppose I was just thrashing out at someone. Carmen didn't tell me anything as such, only that recently Lincoln had been a little distant from her. She put it down to the promotion, but I'm not sure myself. I know I told you to dig deep on him. Did you do that?"

"We did and found nothing. I'm not sure if you think that's a good or bad thing?"

"I'm torn. Damn, I wish I could be more helpful in that respect."

"I didn't ask at the hospital. Were you aware that Carmen was pregnant?"

"No, that was the first I'd heard about it. Maybe that's why I'm an emotional wreck and struggling to deal with things. Because I've not only lost the sister who I adored, but I never got to meet my niece or nephew. That's a very bitter pill to swallow, Inspector."

"I can totally understand how you must feel regarding the baby. Such a travesty to lose both of them that way. Look, I have to get on now, but I want to assure you that I'll be keeping a watchful eye on Lincoln. In fact, I'm going to visit him this afternoon. Perhaps you can tell me the name of the pub he manages in town?"

"It's one of those rowdy places in the town centre. I've not visited it for a while because it's just not my scene. It's called the Watering Hole."

"Brilliant, thanks for that, Jacky. You take care of yourself, and hopefully, I'll be in touch soon with some good news."

"Thank you, Inspector. Maybe that will ease the loss I'm feeling."

Kayli hung up and left her seat. She opened the window wider to try and clear the tiredness that was gnawing at her mind.

Dave stuck his head around the door a few minutes later. "Are you okay? Thought I better check on you in case you had nodded off over your paperwork."

"I'm fine. Just getting a touch of fresh air. How are things going out there?"

"Slowly, very slowly. We've managed to contact about three quarters of the names on the list, but it's been an utter waste of time so far."

"What about Donna? Any luck trying to track down the bike?"

"She's doing well. Has about five names on the list so far. She's in the process of checking; she hasn't overlooked another one, aware of how important that information is to the case."

"She's a treasure. You all are. I know I don't tell you guys that enough."

Dave hitched up a shoulder. "We're all just doing the jobs we're paid to do."

"No, you don't, and you know it, matey. Take today for instance—you must feel as tired as I do, but we're still plodding on."

"It's once in a blue moon, boss. If we didn't love the job, I doubt we'd put ourselves through it. Do you need a coffee to give you an extra kick?"

"I need something. Thanks, that would be great, and then— providing you're up to it—I think we should go and visit Lincoln James."

Dave frowned. "Any specific reason?"

"I've just taken a call from Jacky, and it reminded me that we should still be counting him as a possible person of interest in this enquiry."

"I won't disagree there. Maybe he can point us in the direction of someone who owns a Harley."

"I agree. Right, a quick coffee, then we'll shoot off."

~ ~ ~

Thirty minutes later, Kayli and Dave parked on double yellow lines outside the Watering Hole. "Put the sign on the dashboard to prevent any over-officious traffic wardens from giving us a ticket, Dave."

They left the car and walked into the bar. There were mirrors everywhere, which gave the impression that the room was larger than it actually was. The place was pretty busy, with around fifty customers sitting either at the bar or around the surrounding tables. Kayli wondered if the bar attracted the people working in nearby shops and offices during their lunch hour, although several people appeared to have boutique bags on the floor at their feet. The bar sparkled as they approached it. All the pumps were polished, and the glasses sitting at the back of the bar glinted under the lights. There were four serving bartenders; one of them was Lincoln. He didn't notice Dave and Kayli until he took the money from the customer he was dealing with and looked up to see who was next. His eyes almost popped onto the bar in front of him.

"Hello, Lincoln. We were in the area so thought we'd drop by to see you."

"Oh, right. You've caught me at a busy time."

"We can see that. Maybe you could spare us five minutes in your office?" Kayli asked, her gaze drifting along the bar at the customers sitting along its length. Most of the people were in either groups or pairs. However, there was a lady sitting alone at the end of the bar, whose gaze wandered Kayli's way now and again as she sipped her drink.

"Okay, you win. Fran, cover me while I talk to these people. I'll be in my office if you need me. I shouldn't be too long."

A young woman with dyed scarlet hair nodded and took over serving the customers in Lincoln's area as he walked the length of the bar and exited it. Kayli and Dave strolled in the same direction to meet him.

Lincoln led them through a door, down a narrow corridor, and into a cluttered office. "Excuse the mess. I don't have time to tidy up, as you can imagine. This place is heaving most of the time."

Kayli smiled tautly. "No problem. We've been in worse places than this."

They all took a seat around the dusty desk. "What can I do for you, Inspector?"

"This is just a courtesy call if you like, to see how you're dealing with your loss?"

"I'm lucky in that this place keeps me occupied fifteen hours a day. I deal with my grief after I cash up at the end of my shift. I can tell you it's not easy."

"I can imagine. Maybe it would be better if you took some time off. I'm sure no one would blame you for doing that under the circumstances."

His head dropped, and he stared at the desk. When he looked up again, Kayli noticed the tears welling up in his eyes. "I did take time off to visit her yesterday. You know, at the mortuary."

"I see. Were you able to get some kind of closure from your visit?"

"No, if anything, it made me feel much worse. It enforced upon me how much I've lost, not only Carmen, but the baby, as well. She didn't tell me. I had no idea I was about to become a father. I'm confused by that. Why didn't she tell me?"

"According to her friend Dawn, Carmen was waiting for the right time to present itself. She was going to tell you after she'd had the twelve-week scan. She also wanted you to get used to the idea of her promotion, I believe."

He shook his head in disbelief. "That baby was mine as much as it was hers. I had a right to know."

"There's no denying that. Maybe there was another reason Carmen kept the secret from you."

He frowned. "I have no idea what that might be. I hope you're not suggesting something, Inspector?"

"Not suggesting anything. I'm just offering up a possible answer to your question. Were things okay between you?"

"Yes. We loved each other." His gaze drifted off to the left, indicating that he was lying.

"Did you?" Kayli pushed, her desire to pin him down outweighing her need to treat him with kid gloves, considering he seemed to be going about his daily business as usual.

He glared at her. "What are you insinuating? That I didn't?"

"Merely asking the question. Don't forget, I was there when you had that little contretemps with Jacky at the hospital. That's raised a few questions in my mind, I can tell you."

"Well, it shouldn't. I loved her with all my heart. We had plans to get married next year."

"How far had those plans got?" Kayli challenged.

"Carmen was dealing with everything. It's more a woman's big day rather than the man's, isn't it?" he replied sharply, his eyes narrowing with suspicion. "Wait a minute ... you're not saying that you think I had anything to do with Carmen's death, are you?"

"Until some evidence comes our way to the contrary, we have to keep an open mind on that."

He flung himself back in the chair and interlocked his fingers behind his head. "This is incredible. I don't believe this is happening. I've lost not only my girlfriend, but also my baby, and yet you're intent on flinging this shit at me. What the heck have I done to deserve this? All because her grieving sister lashed out at me? You now see me as some kind of monster who would deliberately drive my girlfriend off the road? It's ludicrous beyond words! I feel I need to remind you that whilst the accident was happening, I was here, and you know something further? I have over a hundred people or more who could vouch for that. I guess you haven't thought through that particular line of questioning thoroughly enough before going down that route, eh, Inspector?"

"Like I said, it's early in the investigation, and everyone involved in the case will be treated as a person of interest."

"I'm sure Jacky doesn't appreciate that, either. Oh wait, by the embarrassed look on your face, I take it you've told a lie there. Jacky is in the clear, am I right?"

Kayli sighed. He was a slick bugger. She'd underestimated him. "No, Jacky isn't being regarded as a suspect in our investigation."

He chewed on the inside of his mouth, and his lips twisted into a sneer. "Do you realise how wrong that is? If you continue to think this way, I'll be forced to issue a complaint to your superiors. Your handling of this case is laughable if you think I could kill Carmen. I repeat, I have a lock-tight alibi. However, according to you, that doesn't seem good enough."

"I didn't say that, Lincoln. There is no point in you getting irate about this, either. All I'm doing is my job at the end of the day." Kayli shrugged. "We've dealt with cases before where a spouse or partner has actually paid someone else to get rid of their partner." She hadn't—she just wanted to gauge his reaction.

Lincoln glanced at Dave and pointed at Kayli. "Jesus, is she for real? How the fuck do you put up with her talking such claptrap day in, day out?"

"Do you want to calm it down, mate? Like the inspector has already stated, if we didn't ask the questions, we wouldn't be doing our jobs properly. There is one question I'd like to ask ..." Dave turned to face Kayli, who nodded, giving him the go-ahead to proceed. "Do you happen to know anyone who rides a Harley-Davidson?"

Lincoln scratched the side of his head. "No. Should I?"

"A bike was seen close to the scene before Carmen hit the barrier."

"Then what are you wasting time questioning me for? You should be out there searching for that damn bike. Bloody hell, are you lot that incompetent you don't see a clue when it's presented to you?" He banged his fists on the desk and stood up. "I think we're done here."

"No. We're not. Sit down, Mr. James, and try and hold on to that temper of yours," Kayli ordered.

Lincoln dropped into his chair, leaned back, and stuck his feet on the edge of the desk. "Go on then, continue with your pathetic questions, wasting my time when I have a super busy business to run."

"That's very generous of you." Kayli sighed. "One last question. Do you happen to know a man called Adam Finley?"

Lincoln bounced upright in his chair and leaned across the table at them, his eyes as wide as headlights. "Yes, I know Adam. What about him? Is he something to do with this?"

Kayli felt Dave's gaze on her. She pressed on regardless of whether her partner felt she was doing the right thing or not. "Adam Finley lost his life last night on the same stretch of road as Carmen."

"He what? You're fucking having me on."

"May I ask how you know Adam?"

"Jesus! He was my best mate."

CHAPTER EIGHT

Kayli looked at Dave sharply then back at Lincoln. "Your best friend?"

"Yes. Oh my God! How can both of them be dead within forty-eight hours of each other?"

"That's what we'd like to know," Dave piped up, a frown of suspicion creasing his brow.

Lincoln fell back in his chair and shook his head. "Jesus, I can't believe this is happening. How did he die? An accident?"

"No. He was the victim of a drive-by shooting."

"He was shot? Here? In Bristol?" he asked, disbelief etched into his expression. Sudden tears sprang to his eyes and toppled onto his cheeks.

Kayli wondered if the man's tears were for their benefit. It struck her as odd that he hadn't shown as much heartache when the doctor announced Carmen's death. *What's your game, buster? Whatever it is you're up to, I intend finding out what it is and soon!*

Dave nudged her leg under the table. "How long have you and Adam been friends?"

"Since secondary school. We went through school together, started going on double dates with the girls in our late teens, and have remained best buddies ever since. I can't believe he'll never walk into my bar again."

"I'm sorry for your loss. Of both Adam and Carmen—we mustn't forget her in this scenario too. As they were both close to you, can you think of anyone who would want to hurt you? Have you made any enemies? Running this place perhaps?"

Lincoln shook his head and stared at her. "No. Not that I can think of. Are you suggesting someone has killed them to get back at me?"

Kayli shrugged. "It wouldn't be the first time we've had to deal with an investigation that went along those lines. Perhaps you can give us a few names of people Adam has fallen out with?"

"No, I can't, because I don't think he ever fell out with anyone, not to my knowledge anyway. He was a great guy, would've given you the last tenner in his wallet if you were in dire straits and needed the money. I can't understand why anyone would intentionally target him. It's unconscionable that someone would do that."

Something just wasn't sitting right with Kayli, but the more she thought about what was irking her about this man, the more frustrated she became. Why hadn't Carmen's and the baby's deaths been as devastating? Was he that heartless? *Yes, he had known Adam longer, but could that really and truly be a reason not so show emotion when the woman you shared your home with suddenly dies?* "Try and think. I know how upsetting this news is for you to take in, but we need you to give us something to go on in order to get this investigation underway."

He shook his head. "I can't think of anyone who would have that much hatred in them to do this, Inspector, and that's the truth. Whether I'll be able to give you a name in a day or two, well, that's a different story. This news has been hard to digest."

"Okay, we'll get on in that case. I'll leave you one of my cards should you think of anyone whom we should speak to." She slid a card across the desk, but he made no attempt to pick it up. Lincoln stood up and walked towards the door. Reluctantly, Kayli and Dave followed him back out to the busy bar. "We'll be in touch soon."

Lincoln nodded but said nothing more.

As Kayli and Dave left the bar, she noticed that Dave was breathing heavily. She didn't tackle him about his anger until they were sitting in the car. "Are you sensing something odd about this, Dave? It's not just me, is it?"

"I know what I'd do if I were in charge of this case."

She raised an inquisitive eyebrow. "Go on, surprise me?"

"I'd haul his arse in for questioning."

Kayli sighed. "On what grounds?"

His mouth twisted as he thought, then he flung his hands up in the air. "I don't know. Obstructing a police enquiry?"

"That wouldn't stack up. He's hardly done that, matey. What are we bloody missing here?"

"I don't know, but it's beginning to tick me off."

"Let's get back to the station. Maybe we're both just too knackered to think straight on this one."

"I don't think that's the case. Maybe we should consider putting a tail on him."

"Surveillance? In the hope of what?" Kayli challenged him.

"Stop asking me questions that my brain is too bloody tired to answer."

"Sorry, that wasn't fair. We've still got a couple of hours before we can call it a day. I think it's too soon to consider putting any kind of surveillance on Lincoln. However, that's not to say that I won't change my mind about doing that in the next few days. We just need more on him. I'm not saying he's the culprit in either crime, but something stinks about this case, and I'm at a loss to know what that something is. I sure hope that alters soon before anyone else connected to Lincoln dies."

"He owns a bar, right?"

Kayli nodded and rolled her eyes. "That's correct."

"Don't look at me like that. Hear me out a second. What if this has to do with some kind of protection racket?"

Kayli contemplated his question for a few moments and nodded. "Well, it's definitely worth looking in to. Do you know of any gangs operating that type of thing in this area?"

"No. We'd need to see what flags up on the system."

"All right, maybe you've hit on something there, but there's something puzzling me about that scenario. Yes, it's feasible that Carmen might have been caught up in something as underhanded as this. What I can't get to grips is why a gang would go after Adam Finley?"

Dave shrugged. "I'm not saying I'm right, but I don't think it's something we should ignore, either. At the end of the day, what else have we got to go on?"

"You're right. Why don't you do some digging into that when we get back?"

"With pleasure."

"I think I'm going to call a press conference for later this afternoon, if I can get one organised that quickly. I just hope I can stay awake long enough to speak in front of the cameras."

"Good idea. Maybe someone can give us a lead on the Harley."

"Perhaps Donna can give us some good news on that when we get back."

CHAPTER NINE

A couple of hours later, Kayli was addressing the local and regional press in its many forms and pleading for the public's assistance. "Please, if you know of anyone who drives a motorbike like this in the area, get in touch with me on the number shown at the bottom of your screen. It's imperative we locate the person immediately." She held a blown-up photo of the bike from the CCTV footage. "If you were on the B4054 on either of the nights in question and saw this bike, or if you saw it on any of the roads leading off the B-road, please, please let us know. It's important we track this person down immediately. One last thing, we have limited resources, and our officers cannot be on every street twenty-four seven. Therefore, we're relying on you being our eyes and ears on the street. I want to assure you that we're doing our utmost to apprehend this person, but until we do, I'm imploring you to take care, especially at night." Kayli knew that if the DCI heard her briefing, she would be annoyed by Kayli's use of such scare tactics on the public. However, needs must in Kayli's eyes, and if the ruse worked, then it would make their lives a whole lot easier. She left the room, the media murmuring their surprise behind her.

When she walked through the reception area, the desk sergeant motioned that he wanted a word with her. "What's up, Ray?"

He thumbed over his shoulder at a well-dressed man in his early forties pacing the floor. "I have someone requesting to see you, ma'am."

"Does this person have a name?" Kayli asked, eyeing the man warily.

"A Brian Finley."

Kayli smiled. "Ah, yes, I've been expecting him. Is there an interview room available? I'd rather not take him up to my office with the evidence board on view."

"Of course. They're all available. It's a quiet day on the petty crime front."

"Thanks. I'll collect him and opt for Room One in that case." She walked towards the man with an outstretched arm. "Hello, there, Mr. Finley, I'm DI Kayli Bright. We spoke on the phone. Thank you for coming to see me so promptly. If you'd like to follow me."

"Hello, Inspector. I got here as fast as I could. I thought I'd drop in here first before I visit Adam at the mortuary. I should be able to see him today, shouldn't I?"

"It might be too soon for that, but I can certainly ring the pathologist to find out for you." Kayli led the way up the hallway.

"I'd appreciate that."

Kayli gestured for Brian to take a seat at the table. "Have you seen Anita yet?"

"Yes, briefly. Her friend Mandy ended up asking a doctor to come out and give her something to help her sleep. She was very woozy. Tell me, have you got any idea who the offender is yet?"

"No. I've just held a press conference, asking for the public's help to identify the vehicle we picked up on CCTV footage."

"Let's hope something comes of it. Are you dealing with any other incidences of this nature, Inspector?"

"Okay, I don't usually open up to victims' families during an investigation. However, my partner and I found out something very interesting this afternoon that could link your brother's death to another crime we're investigating."

"Are you going to tell me what that crime is, Inspector? Is it another shooting? What's the connection exactly?"

"Before I answer your questions, can you tell me if you know a Lincoln James?"

"Yes, of course I know Lincoln. He was Adam's best friend. Has been since they were at school together. Why?"

Kayli exhaled a large breath. "Because the night before your brother was killed, Lincoln's girlfriend died in a fatal accident. We believe that someone is guilty of forcing her off the road, the B4054, and causing her death and that of her unborn child."

His hands covered his face then pushed his grey hair back off his forehead. "What? I don't believe this! How? Is the connection Lincoln?" he asked, his solicitor's brain swiftly kicking into action.

"We didn't think so at first. Now, in light of the fact that Lincoln knew both the victims, we're inclined to believe he's the connection, although we've only just realised this and have yet to delve deeper into why."

"You're not suggesting he's a suspect, are you?"

"I don't see the point in lying to you, given your profession, Brian. Let's just say I'm keeping a very open mind on that for now."

He expelled a breath and shook his head. "I find that incredible to believe. However, I understand why you must investigate this angle."

"How well do you know Lincoln yourself?"

"Fairly well. He used to stay over at the house when they were at school. I'd moved out by then, being six years older than Adam. What I do know is that my parents treated Lincoln like another son. They'll be devastated to think you're regarding him as a suspect."

"I'm not, yet. Please don't let this conversation go any further."

"I won't. Look, Inspector, all I want is for you to find the person responsible for putting my brother in the mortuary. I still think you're barking up the wrong tree if you end up accusing Lincoln of the crime. What would be his motive, for a start?"

Kayli shook her head. "We haven't discovered one as yet. If you can vouch for his character, then that's good enough for me. Did Adam ever mention if he had any enemies?"

"No. He's such a genuinely friendly guy. He bore the good genes in the family. Always remained even-tempered no matter what was thrown at him, unlike me. I tend to strike out first—with a tongue-lashing, I mean, never with my fists—and ask questions later."

"I'm the same. Maybe that's due to the careers we've chosen. I asked the same question of Lincoln a few hours ago. If anything, I'm leaning towards someone maybe having a problem with him and seeking revenge by targeting those closest to him."

He nodded. "And what was Lincoln's reaction to that?"

"He was inconsolable about Adam's death and unable to give me any information that could spark us into investigating that side of things. I've left my card with him in the hope that he snaps out of his grief soon and puts his thinking cap on, if you like. Our investigation is at a standstill until he can provide us with some useful information."

"Would it help if I dropped by to see him?"

She shook her head. "By what you've just told me about giving people a tongue-lashing, maybe you should sit on that for a day or two. I'm sure something will come from the appeal I've just put out.

Fingers crossed, anyway. We're trying to trace all the people in the area who own a Harley-Davidson. That's the bike we've spotted on CCTV footage around the time both incidents occurred."

"There can't be that many in the area, surely?"

"I don't think there are. Our problem is that the number plate was deliberately obscured. For all we know, the bike might be housed in a garage and not see the light of day until it gets dark, if you get my meaning."

"I do. I don't envy you the task of tracking the vehicle down, given the facts you've just presented." He smiled. "Sorry for the solicitor speak."

"I'm glad you understand our dilemma. Not everyone will with this case. We're doing our best with the evidence that has surfaced so far. I must tell you one thing, but this mustn't go any further." He nodded. "I have a feeling there is more to Lincoln than we've managed to ascertain so far. I was at the hospital when Carmen lost her life, and I witnessed the reaction Carmen's sister, Jacky, had towards Lincoln. It's been niggling at me ever since."

"I don't understand. He's always been pleasant enough to me. Of course, I lost contact with him a few years ago when I moved north. Did you question the sister?"

"As much as I could without seeming to be insensitive after her sister's death."

"I see. I take it you've carried out a background check on Lincoln?"

Kayli nodded.

"Of course you have."

"We've found nothing. I didn't really expect to because he has a liquor licence. You know how stringent the searches are to obtain one of those?"

"I do. Maybe he's in the clear, and it's your investigative imagination getting the better of you. I realise we've only just met, but you seem a pretty astute woman, Inspector. Maybe a little too astute." He laughed lightly.

Kayli smiled. "Maybe you're right. My partner has taken over the reins of looking into the Lincoln side of things, so maybe by distancing myself from him my thinking will become clearer. Anyway, if there's nothing else, I better get back to see if the appeal has prompted any calls into the incident room."

"No, there's nothing else. Thank you for taking the time out of your exhaustive schedule to speak with me. If I can just ask a small favour of you before you go?"

She frowned and tilted her head. "What's that?"

"You mentioned that you could clear things with the pathologist for me."

"Of course." She fished her phone out of her pocket and dialled the mortuary's number.

Naomi wasn't available, but one of her assistants said that Adam Finley's body was in the process of being prepared for the family viewing. Kayli thanked the assistant and ended the call. "She asked that you give them half an hour or so, if that's okay?"

"I appreciate that. Thank you, Inspector. It'll give me enough time to freshen up before I pay my final respects to my brother." His eyes became moist, and he brushed at them with the back of his hand.

Why do some men consider breaking down and showing their emotions a sign of weakness?

Kayli rose from her chair and walked towards the door. "I'll show you out. I've got your number. As soon as I have a suspect under arrest, I'll ring you—you have my word on that."

They strode up the corridor side-by-side.

"I appreciate that. Give me a call if you need anything. Good luck, Inspector." He shook her hand firmly, which was unusual for a man. Normally men felt they needed to be gentle with her slim fingers so as not to crush them.

"I will. Be in touch soon." She watched him walk out of the building before she turned on her heel and ran up the stairs to the incident room. As she neared the door, she heard several phones ringing. She punched the air in excitement and entered the room to find all three members of her team on the phone. *At last! Let's hope something breaks soon.*

Dave glanced up at her and shook his head, followed by Donna and Graeme, both of whom gave her a negative response.

Dave hung up. "I think you scared the whole of Bristol into ringing us. We're not getting the leads we need to aid the investigation. All we're getting is a lot of hassle from people demanding that we get out there and track this bike and its driver down."

Kayli slammed her clenched fist against her thigh. "Shit! That wasn't my intention. Sorry, guys. Lesson learned: there's a fine line between asking the public for information and scaring the crap out of them, and I think I've just overstepped that mark."

"All's not lost yet, boss," Donna said. "I've had a few calls mentioning the names and addresses of people who have motorbikes. I'm going to tally those up with the names already on my list. I'll get back to you with the results in a few minutes."

"Thanks, Donna. At least that sounds more hopeful. Our next step should be seeking out these people who own the Harleys and either ask them to come in for questioning or go and visit them."

"What if the offender is among those on the list? If we make contact, he could run," Dave said.

Kayli shrugged. "I'm open to suggestions, Dave."

He sat back in his chair and tapped the side of his face with his pen. "I don't know what the answer is. Maybe get uniform to drive by the addresses and see if they're a match?"

"I know nothing about motorbikes, but wouldn't they all look the same?"

Graeme nodded. "Sort of. They can vary from model to model. I've been in touch with a motorbike expert I know, and he's going to try and identify the model for me from the picture. It doesn't help that the number plate was obscured, though. The thing is, the driver could easily clean the plates up after he's done the deed. So would there be any point sending uniform out to the addresses? Again, if our guys are spotted, the offender could still take off."

Kayli stared at the wall ahead of her for a moment, trying to solve the problem, but nothing came to mind. "Let's stick with gathering the evidence from the calls for now and revisit the situation later. Let me know what your friend says. I'll be in my office if you need me. Just grin and bear any flack coming your way from the public on this one, guys."

Disappointed that she had apparently caused the team extra work, she walked into her office and shut the door. She could hear the phones in the incident room starting up again. *A bloody nightmare if nothing comes from this.*

An hour and a half, and the beginnings of a headache, later, Kayli rejoined the team for an update. "How does it look?" she asked, walking towards Dave's desk.

"Donna has matched a couple of the calls to the Harley list. Apart from that, the motorbikes people are ringing in about are not Harleys."

Kayli sighed, feeling beat down by the news. "Damn! Saying that, I don't think I'd be able to name the different makes of bikes out there, and I certainly couldn't identify them."

"Not so fast. Graeme's friend thinks he can identify the model of the bike. Don't laugh ... it's called a Fat Boy Lo, 2010 model."

"That's brilliant news and done wonders for my spirit."

"Where do we go from here then, boss?"

Weariness replacing her sudden high, Kayli perched on the desk behind her and rubbed at her temples to try to ease the pain in her pounding head. "Although I'd love to go home and put my feet up, I think we should visit the owners of the Harleys. How many have we got in the immediate vicinity, Donna?"

"Five, boss."

"That's not too many. What about if we leave Donna here to answer the phone and the three of us visit the owners?"

Dave shrugged, and Graeme nodded.

"And what do we say when we arrive at the addresses?" Graeme asked, puzzled.

"I suppose see if the bike is on show first of all, Graeme. Give it a discreet look over and then ask the driver how often he uses it and which route he takes. Don't ask anything too invasive at this point. Let's head off. Dave and I will call at two addresses each, and Graeme, you stick with the fifth one. It shouldn't take us too long."

The three of them left the station together and returned a few hours later, feeling like they'd wasted their time. Three of the bikes' owners were at work in their day-to-day vehicles, according to their wives. They had persuaded the wives to show them the bikes sitting in the garage, but it was clear that those weren't the ones they were interested in. The other two bikes, the owners had taken to work with them. Graeme and Dave checked at the workplace of each of the owners and, again, soon realised the bikes weren't the one connected to the crime."

Kayli asked Donna and Graeme to stay on later than usual to answer any calls that would likely come in from the evening news bulletin that was due to air in a couple of hours. However, she and Dave called it a day at five thirty. On her way out of the station, she confirmed with the desk sergeant that there would be a few cars patrolling the B4054 during the night.

She rang the bell at Annabelle's house twenty minutes later, dead on her feet since the day's adrenaline had subsided.

Annabelle kissed her cheek and offered her a glass of wine without hesitation.

"That would be great. It's been a very looong day."

"You're not kidding. How often does that type of thing happen?"

Kayli sat down at the kitchen table and sipped her glass of chilled white wine. "Not that often, thankfully. I know the public are always slating us for not patrolling the streets like we used to, but when you pull long shifts such as Dave and I did today, something has to give. I think my team and I gave it our all today. I'm satisfied, anyway."

"And have you managed to arrest anyone yet? I caught the appeal this afternoon. You looked so frustrated."

"That's what is bugging me the most. It is such a frustrating case—they both are. We did stumble across something today that I think will lead the investigation in a different direction."

"Sounds intriguing. Are you going to share or leave me dangling?" Annabelle grinned, raising an eyebrow.

After another sip of wine, Kayli relaxed into her chair. "The first victim's boyfriend was also best friends with the second victim."

"Wow! Are you thinking the boyfriend is behind both crimes?"

Kayli shook her head. "I suppose most officers would go down that route. I'm thinking more along the lines that someone has deliberately set out to punish him by venting their anger on those close to him."

"Blimey, your police brain really takes you on a wondrous journey at times, doesn't it?"

Kayli chuckled. "It definitely does. We'll be keeping an eye on this guy all the same. We've been conned before. What's for dinner? Shall we get another takeaway?"

Annabelle placed her hand over her heart. "I'm mortified that you should say that. Can't you smell it?"

Kayli sniffed the air. "Sorry, too exhausted even to do that today. I can smell it now. What is it?"

"Cottage pie with a twist."

"Sounds intriguing. What's the twist? It won't be ready until ten tonight?"

Annabelle laughed. "You're a scream. No, actually, I'm not going to tell you. It's one of Giles's favourites." Her head dropped to her chest, and Kayli covered Annabelle's hand with her own.

"They'll be home in a few days. Let's not get all maudlin about this. Hey, did you get your results?"

Annabelle looked up with watery eyes and nodded. "It was confirmed. You're going to be an auntie again."

Kayli leapt out of her chair and hugged her sister-in-law. "Spectacular news. I'm sure Giles will be over the moon when you tell him."

"I hope so. I thought maybe we could arrange another family barbeque over the weekend. I could keep him in the dark until then and announce it to everyone. What do you think?"

"Brilliant idea. I'll give Mum a ring. She revels in a good family get-together."

"Do it after dinner. I'm going to dish up now. I can't remember if you like cauliflower or not?"

"I do. Did you manage to get any sleep yourself during the day?"

Annabelle removed the plates from one of the cupboards and placed them at the bottom of the oven to warm up. "I catnapped. Bobby has been on top form today, vying for my attention most of the day. I was relieved when he zonked out just before you got home. No doubt he'll make an unwanted appearance later."

"Crikey, I think once I've had dinner, I'll be falling into bed soon. Not sure how I'm managing to keep my eyes open, to be honest."

"Dinner will revitalise you. I can guarantee that."

Kayli narrowed her eyes. "I'm detecting there's a little spice in this secret recipe of yours."

Annabelle gave an innocent shrug before she pulled the dish from the oven. "My lips are sealed. Don't judge it until you've tasted it."

Kayli peered over her sister-in-law's shoulder as she served up the food. The smell was heavenly. "That looks delicious. You're such a good cook. I get by with the dinners I make, but my attempts are pretty dismal in comparison to your results. I can't wait to try it. Why is the topping so yellow?"

"Let's hope we both enjoy it. I won't be offended if you leave some, okay? I've made enough to feed a small refugee camp."

Kayli's phone rang before she could reply. "Hi, Mum, how's it diddling? I was going to ring you later."

"Hello, dear. Just thought I'd ring up to see how you are. I won't keep you long if you're about to eat. What were you going to ring me about?"

"I'm at Annabelle's. And yes, she's just about to dish up dinner. The boys are due home on Friday, I thought maybe we could have a family barbeque over the weekend at your place. We'll all chip in, of course."

"How wonderful! What a fabulous idea! Nonsense, your father and I will handle everything. Shall we say Sunday?"

"Sunday would be great, Mum."

"Good. Okay, I have lots to prepare before then. Say hello to Annabelle and that gorgeous grandson of mine. I'll love you and leave you to get on with your meal, darling."

"I'll do that, Mum. See you Sunday. Say hi to Dad for me."

"I will. Goodbye, dear."

Kayli hung up as Annabelle deposited the plates on the table. She took a moment to observe the plateful of food. "Is that bolognaise?"

Annabelle laughed. "Stop scrutinising it and tuck in."

She savoured her first mouthful. Different spices and tastes exploded in her mouth. Annabelle watched her with trepidation etched on her face. "Good Lord, I think I've died and gone to heaven. How on earth did you come up with this concoction?"

"Simple. I had some leftover bolognaise sauce one time and wondered what I could do with it. Giles suggested using sweet potato for the topping, and then I came up with adding breadcrumbs and cheese to finish it off."

"Wow, it's delicious. If this doesn't give us our appetite back, then nothing will. My compliments to the chef."

They devoured the delicious meal, cleaned up the kitchen, then went through to the lounge and collapsed on the couch, Kayli with her glass of wine and Annabelle with her glass of apple juice. The conversation flowed until both of them started to feel the effects of their long days. At eight o'clock, and with Bobby still fast asleep, they decided to give in and go to bed.

Sleep came quickly. The glass of wine she'd downed had likely helped, but Kayli was woken up at ten past four by her mobile ringing. Dazed, she answered the call. "Hello, DI Bright."

"Sorry to disturb you again, ma'am, at such an early hour"—the tone of the control room operator's voice made her stomach clench—"but we've had another shooting incident."

"Okay, I'm fully awake now. Where?"

"In the centre of Bristol on Temple Way."

"Damn. Another drive-by? Was there a bike involved?"

"Yes, to both those questions, ma'am. The pathologist and her team are at the scene. Will you be attending?"

"Try and stop me. I'll be there in approximately thirty minutes. Do me a favour and relay that information to the pathologist on call and ring my partner, Dave Chaplin—no, wait. On second thoughts, leave him out of this one. I'll assess the scene myself and ring him from there if I need him."

"Yes, ma'am. Thank you."

Kayli ended the call and rushed into the bathroom to have a quick wash. She regretted not showering before she'd fallen into bed, but truthfully, she'd been too exhausted to do even that. She hunted through the bag she'd left at Annabelle's the previous evening and pulled out a slightly creased blouse and a pair of black trousers and slipped them on. After running a comb through her long hair, she tied it in a ponytail and was out the door, sitting behind the wheel of her car, within ten minutes of receiving the call.

CHAPTER TEN

It was drizzling heavily when she dipped under the cordon tape at the scene. As Kayli walked towards Naomi and the rest of her team, the pathologist pointed to the rear of her car. "You'll need to don the paper," she said, meaning the white paper suit they wore to keep from contaminating the scene.

"As per. I'll be right back. Are you putting up a marquee?"

Naomi tagged along with her. "No point. The incident took place inside the woman's car."

"Any ID on her yet?"

"Yes, I found her bag untouched in the footwell on the passenger side. Her driving licence indicates that she is Brenda Godfrey, fifty-five years old and local."

"Damn, another woman! Not that it makes one jot of difference if the victims are male or female, but you know what I mean."

"I do. Shocking. I reckon the offender pulled up on his bike alongside her and shot her through the passenger window. She didn't stand a chance." Naomi pointed at the traffic lights. "Maybe there's a traffic camera to corroborate my theory."

"Don't worry. That's usually my first port of call. Why? It seems such a senseless act to pick out a member of the public like that ... unless the offender knows the victim."

"Of course there's a good chance of that ... Is there something you're not telling me, Kayli?"

Kayli zipped up the suit and motioned for Naomi to lead the way back to the crime scene. "Something came to light during the investigation yesterday. The first victim's boyfriend knew both victims."

"Interesting. I suppose he'll be the first person you'll contact about this victim then, right?"

"Yep, it's a no-brainer. Damn. I need to get this bastard off the road. The people of Bristol are already coming down heavily on me and my team."

"It's hardly your fault if you haven't caught this guy yet. He could be carrying out the hits and then covering his tracks really well."

"Wait a minute ... How do we know a bike was involved?"

Naomi's neck disappeared into her hitched shoulders. "Sorry, I should have said, there's a witness over there."

Kayli's eyes found a young man talking to a uniformed officer under the protection of a nearby tree. "Excellent. Do you mind if I have a word with him first?"

"Go for it. I'm not going anywhere for a while yet."

Kayli punched her fist against Naomi's. "I'll be back in a jiffy." Glancing into the car as she passed, Kayli winced. There was blood all over the windscreen. The woman had been shot in the head. Barely managing to hang on to the remains of the delicious dinner Annabelle had served up, she approached the witness and the officer, who stood aside once she'd introduced herself.

"Hello, ma'am, this is Stuart Nicholls, who witnessed the incident," the constable said.

"Thanks, Constable. Hello, sir. I'm very sorry you had to witness such a dreadful crime. Can you run through what you actually saw?"

The man's eyes were bulbous with trauma. "I was driving on the other side of the road. The lights had just turned green. These lights were red, and the woman's car had pulled up. Not sure what made me look her way, but when I did, I noticed a Harley-Davidson draw up alongside her. He extracted a weapon from his coat and blasted her through the passenger window. Shit! Why would someone do that? She was just minding her own business, sitting there waiting for the lights to change," he rattled off his account rapidly.

"I have no idea, but I intend finding out. What happened next?"

"The driver looked around, saw me, and put his foot down. The lights were still red, and he was lucky no one was coming in the other direction. Otherwise, he would have been hit. As soon as I thought he was out of sight, I stopped my car and ran across the road. I was going to try and help the woman. I was too late, though. She was already dead."

"It was good of you to stop. Most people would rather not get involved."

"The thought crossed my mind, Inspector. Don't worry about that. Had the driver not driven off and remained at the scene, gloating at his work, I would have continued on my route and rung you from farther up the road."

"We appreciate you calling us. Can you give us any details about the driver?"

"I've just told the officer. He was wearing a silver helmet that shielded his face from me, so I can't give you any more details on that front. He had on a red zipped-up leather jacket and wore black leather trousers—at least I think they were black. Not quite sure in this light, and I only got a brief glimpse."

"That's brilliant. Hopefully, the traffic camera will be able to give us a close-up of this individual. Thank you for calling us." Kayli turned to the constable. "Can you continue taking down Mr. Nicholls's official statement?"

"Yes, ma'am."

Kayli extended her hand to Mr. Nicholls. "Thank you, sir. We'll be in touch if we need anything else."

"My pleasure. I hope you get this lunatic off the road soon."

"So do I," she said before turning and walking back to Naomi.

Her pathologist friend was inside the car, extracting pieces of evidence from the dashboard and from the woman's head.

Kayli crouched beside Naomi, forcing herself to look at the victim. "Have you found the bullet?"

"Bullets, you mean? Yes, there are a few here. Definite overkill to me."

"As if the victim is known to the offender?"

"In my experience, yes, that would be my assumption."

"Shit! I need to get on to Lincoln James first thing to see if he knows her, in that case. A bloody mindless act whether he knows her or not. If it is connected, we're in the serial killer territory now, and by the looks of things, his crimes are becoming more heinous. Whatever next?"

"My suggestion would be lock down the city."

Kayli snorted and shook her head. "Like that's about to happen. I'd do it in a heartbeat, but I can't see that suggestion going down too well with my superiors. I'll have a word with my DCI, see what she thinks. Any idea what kind of gun?"

"I don't see many gunshot wounds. I'll need to get a second opinion from a specialist when I get back. I'll let you know later."

"The witness said she was dead before he got to her."

"Not surprised. She would have died instantly for sure. I'll be another half an hour or so, and then I'll get her transported back to the lab."

"Okay, let me know when you can. I'll go to the station, see if I can organise the CCTV footage. Hopefully, that will flag up something we can sink our teeth into. If not, we're screwed again."

Naomi looked her way and smiled. "Good luck with your DCI."

"Thanks, I'm going to need it. I'll leave my suit beside your vehicle."

"Okay, I'll be in touch soon."

Kayli stripped off the suit and left it lying in a heap outside Naomi's car. On heavy legs, she walked over to her own vehicle and slipped behind the wheel. She placed her head on the steering wheel, feeling distraught that another person had lost her life—the third in the past seventy-two hours. *Pull yourself together, girl. We have to catch the bastard causing all this havoc and swiftly.*

CHAPTER ELEVEN

By the time the rest of the team arrived at work, Kayli had sourced the CCTV footage. She instructed her colleagues to gather around while she walked them through what had occurred overnight.

"Jesus, another one?" Dave asked, shaking his head in disgust. "What time did you get the call?"

"Around four this morning. Let's watch the footage carefully, see if we can pick out something useful." Kayli hit a key on the keyboard, and the footage began playing. She winced, wishing she'd shielded her eyes when the bullets struck the woman's head and it exploded.

"Jesus! What the fuck! This guy is a nutjob," Dave said, his face paling.

"I agree, which is why we need to get him off the road and soon. Can you tell what type of gun it is, guys?"

Dave and Graeme shook their heads, and Donna shrugged.

"The pathologist thinks the victim was known to the offender again. I didn't see any recognition such as a wave, but then would she have known who it was with him wearing a helmet? Maybe she didn't know the offender rode a bike. The victim looked a tad confused to me."

"I agree," Dave said. "What time did the incident occur?"

Kayli leaned in to view the time on the screen. "Just after two in the morning."

"What was the woman doing out at that time of the morning?"

"Either going to or coming home from work, perhaps. We won't know that until we've spoken to the next of kin. Donna, can you find out the details for me?"

"Want me to start on that now, boss?"

"Yes, please. Dave and I should visit them ASAP. I also need to have a word with the DCI first thing." Kayli swept a stray hair behind her ear.

"Why don't Graeme and I go and see the next of kin while you deal with the DCI?" Dave suggested.

Kayli's inner control freak screamed that she didn't want to go down that route, but then she chastised herself and relinquished. "Good idea. Be gentle, though, Dave."

He tutted. "Despite what you think, I can be caring and sensitive when the need arises."

"Sorry, didn't mean to cast aspersions, Dave. I know you can. All right, let's get this show on the road. Wish me luck with the DCI."

"Luck!" the three other team members shouted as she left the room and started the journey along the corridor to her boss's office. Fiona frowned and looked down at her diary when Kayli entered the room.

"I don't have an appointment, but it is urgent," Kayli said. "Any chance she can squeeze me in?"

Fiona smiled and left her chair. She tapped on the DCI's door and entered the room when she was summoned. "DI Bright to see you on an urgent matter if you can spare the time, ma'am?"

"Very well. Show her in, and hold all my calls for the next fifteen minutes," DCI Davis replied abruptly.

Fiona stepped away from the door and gestured for Kayli to enter the room.

"Sorry to disturb you, DCI Davis."

"Come in and sit down, DI Bright. Is there something wrong? You look like shit, if you don't mind me saying."

Kayli stopped dead in her tracks. She hadn't been expecting the DCI to be so blunt about her personal appearance. She continued to walk to the seat and dropped into it. "Thanks for that boost to my confidence. It would be nice to get some sleep, but duty calls and all that. I started work at one a.m. yesterday and was back on duty at four a.m. this morning."

"I wasn't aware of that. Had I been aware, then I would have kept my opinion to myself. I take it your heavy workload is to do with the case you're working on?"

"That's right, ma'am. We're now looking at three murders within the last seventy-two hours."

DCI Davis's demeanour faltered for the briefest of moments as she fidgeted in her chair. "That's very unfortunate. Do you have any leads?"

"Not yet. The only things linking the first two crimes are the bike and the fact that both victims knew Lincoln James. We're unsure if the latest victim is connected to Mr. James, but the bike was certainly involved. I intend ringing Mr. James in a few minutes to ask the question."

"Are you saying that you believe he's behind the murders?"

"No, that's the problem—I don't believe he is, although something isn't sitting right with me. I can't for the life of me uncover what it is that is bugging me. Background checks have brought up nothing. My thinking is that someone has some kind of vendetta against him and they're intent on punishing those around him."

"Have you suggested that theory to him?"

Kayli nodded. "Yes, he seemed genuine enough when he told me he couldn't figure out who would do such a thing, and according to him, he hasn't fallen out with anyone lately."

"How strange. I suppose it's early days with the latest victim?"

"It is. I've sent two of my team to inform the victim's next of kin. Dave's leading that side of things and will ask if the victim had a connection with Lincoln James. Until we receive the response, we're none the wiser."

"So what next? Do you need something from me, Inspector?"

Kayli inhaled a large breath then let it out slowly as she thought. "More resources. I know the likelihood of that happening is zilch, but we now have a dangerous serial killer on our patch, ma'am. Talking to the pathologist this morning, she thinks we should lock down the city."

DCI Davis jolted upright in her chair, and a little tic began at the corner of her right eye. "Well, that's not going to happen. The pathologist needs to concentrate on her job and let us proceed with ours."

"While I don't entirely agree with her, ma'am, we do need to come up with something that will work in our favour. I've already got the night patrols on the street keeping an eye on the B4054, the location where the first two crimes were committed."

"Good idea. Are you telling me that the third crime took place elsewhere?"

"Yes. In the city at Temple Way. Whether the killer realised the B4054 was being watched, I have no idea."

"It's a pretty big area for our division to patrol. I can see what I can do about getting you extra help, but I'll have to run that past the superintendent first. He'll have to sign it off."

"As long as he doesn't come down heavily on me for not being capable of doing my job. You know I've never asked for help in solving a case before, ma'am."

"Don't worry. Leave him to me. I have confidence in you and your abilities as an inspector. That is not an issue with me. Is there anything else I can do for you?"

"Apart from to arrange for the Armed Response Teams in the area to be put on standby, no, nothing, ma'am."

"Well, they're always on alert. Nonetheless, I'll definitely make them aware of the situation and mention your name as a contact."

"Thank you. I appreciate it, ma'am."

"Very well. Keep me abreast of the investigation from now on, Inspector."

"I'll do that, ma'am. Thank you." She left her chair and walked towards the door.

"Oh, Inspector, one last thing."

"Yes, ma'am?" Kayli asked, looking over her shoulder.

"Take care of yourself. If things begin to feel like they're overwhelming you, then let me know."

"I will, ma'am. The only thing this case is doing so far is frustrating the hell out of me." Kayli closed the door behind her and sighed heavily.

"That bad, eh?" Fiona asked.

"Not really. I suppose it could have been a lot worse. Thanks for squeezing me in."

"No problem. Good luck with the case, Inspector."

When Kayli returned to the incident room, Donna was waiting for her, eyes wide with excitement.

"Tell me they've found the bastard?"

Donna shook her head. "Not quite as good as that, boss."

"Come on, Donna, you know I hate being kept in suspense."

"They think they've found the bike."

"What? Who? Where?"

Donna smiled. "The control room just took a call from a fisherman who spotted the bike at the bottom of the river. Maybe the killer dumped it in the dark after last night's attack, not realising how shallow the river was."

"That's excellent news. I need to get over there and see for myself. Shit! Dave's out there already on another mission. I'll just have to go by myself."

"Want me to ring him? Tell him to meet you at the location once he's finished?"

"Yes, that makes sense. What doesn't make sense is why the killer would dump the bike."

"Maybe he discovered he had a conscience after he'd killed the last victim."

"You could be right, Donna. Give me the location, and I'll make a move. So much for having the time to shove a coffee down my neck," she grumbled, throwing a wishful look at the vending machine.

Donna handed her a Post-it with the address, and she set off straight away.

"Don't forget to ring Dave!" Kayli shouted before she left the room.

CHAPTER TWELVE

When Kayli arrived at the scene, crime scene tape already surrounded the riverfront. A uniformed officer was chatting to a man wearing waterproofs: the fisherman who had made the call, Kayli suspected.

She approached the two men. "Hi, I'm DI Kayli Bright. Can you tell me what happened, sir?"

"I'm Ross Lynch. I was fishing in my usual spot. I usually get here about sixish, as I find I catch more fish at that time of the morning. Anyway, as the dawn broke, something caught my eye in the water. I saw the appeal go out yesterday about a Harley-Davidson and rung the police right away."

"And you didn't notice the bike on any other occasions?"

"No, it definitely wasn't there yesterday. Look at it—it's in too good a nick to have been in the water more than a few hours."

"That's good enough for me. I'll leave you to take down Mr. Lynch's statement, Constable." She smiled at the two men then marched towards the bike that two Scenes of Crime Officers were examining. "Anything of use yet, guys?"

The eldest of the two men shook his head. "Looks like someone has tried their hardest to make life difficult for us."

"In what way?" Kayli frowned then tapped the side of her head with her fist. "Never mind, I see the licence plates have been removed."

"That's just the start of it. The serial number has been scratched out."

"Damn. Will you guys be able to still decipher it?"

The older technician smiled and wiggled his eyebrows. "We have ways of overcoming such vandalism. It'll have to wait until we're back at the lab, though."

"Brilliant. Can you get the results back to me ASAP? The quicker we can get this shit in a cell, the better."

"Agreed. Leave it with us. There's no reason we shouldn't be able to get a result for you by the end of the day—if all goes according to plan, that is."

"Excellent news. I doubt there's going to be DNA left on the bike, if it's been in water," Kayli said.

"No, that is very unlikely. However, we'll do our best. There might be an odd fibre left on the bodywork here and there."

"See what you can do. That's all I can ask." Kayli turned when she heard a car screech to a halt behind her. Dave and Graeme rushed across the grassy area to join her.

"That's it?" Dave pointed at the motorbike still dripping water onto the grass.

"Yep, but it's been vandalised to prevent us from getting an ID on it. The guys are hopeful they'll be able to come up with something useful by the end of the day. How did you two get on?"

His gaze still locked on the bike, Dave replied, "We spoke to the husband. Yes, he was distraught."

"I can imagine. Did you manage to establish what she was doing out at that time of the morning?"

"She'd been babysitting at her daughter's house while her daughter and her husband went out to celebrate their wedding anniversary. She was driving home when the incident occurred."

"Damn. Hate it when that happens. Okay, did you ask the husband if his wife knew Lincoln James?"

Dave nodded, drawing his attention away from the bike to look at her. "I did. He really wasn't sure. But said he was finding it exceedingly difficult to concentrate on my questions in light of what had happened."

"Understandable. I think I'll drop by the bar." Kayli glanced at her watch; it was almost eleven thirty. "Lincoln should be there by now. Why don't you two head back to the station, and I'll return once I've questioned James."

"Are you sure you don't want me to tag along?" Dave asked.

"If you want. Are you going to trust Graeme to drive your car?"

"I thought he could drive *your* car back to the station," Dave shot back promptly.

"Did you? That was a mistake on your part, partner. Hand your keys over."

"I could always flag down a taxi," Graeme volunteered.

Dave reluctantly handed over the keys to his vehicle. "Be gentle with her. She's not as suped-up as yours for a reason, mate."

Graeme chuckled and took the keys. "I'll treat her as if she's just come off the forecourt, mate."

Kayli shook her head at their banter and headed towards her car. "When you two have quite finished, we have an important case to solve. See you in a little while, Graeme. Any scratches on Dave's car, and you'll have me to deal with, got that?"

"Message received, boss." Graeme jumped behind the steering wheel and started up the engine. He revved the throttle a few times, just to get Dave's back up.

"Bastard. He better treat her well," Dave complained under his breath.

"He will. He's winding you up. To my knowledge, he's never had an accident whilst on duty."

Dave turned and raised an eyebrow. "There's always a first time."

Laughing, Kayli tapped his arm. "Come on, we're wasting time. Get in the car."

They parked on double yellow lines outside the Watering Hole around ten minutes later. The bar was quieter than it'd been during their previous visit. They found Lincoln James at the end of the bar, having a discussion with a young woman who was terribly familiar. After wracking her brain for a few minutes, Kayli still couldn't place her. When Lincoln saw Dave and Kayli, his smile dropped.

"Hello, Inspector. To what do I owe the pleasure?" he said, approaching them. He leaned forward and asked quietly, "Have you found the person responsible for killing Carmen and Adam yet?"

"Not yet. Our enquiries are ongoing, Lincoln. Mind if we have a quiet word in your office?"

"Sure, let me get someone to cover." He summoned one of the bartenders from around the other side of the bar and joined Kayli and Dave at the entrance to his office.

Once inside, they all took a seat. Kayli watched the man's expression carefully as she disclosed why they were there. "Do you know a Brenda Godfrey, Lincoln?"

"Let me think. The name isn't ringing any bells. Should I know her?"

"The lady lost her life last night."

His brow creased, and he scratched the side of his face. "What? And you think there's a connection to Carmen and Adam's deaths?"

"Yes, we're connecting all three deaths because this lady was also killed by someone on a Harley-Davidson. Are you sure you don't know the lady or anyone who rides a Harley?"

"No. I've never heard of the woman. Do you have a photo of her?"

"Not yet. The crime scene photo would have been too gruesome to have bandied around. I could ask the lady's husband for a photo if you like?"

"Maybe she comes in the bar a lot. I definitely don't recognise the name, sorry."

"It was worth a shot." Kayli cringed, realising she'd mentioned the word *shot*.

"So you think this person is guilty of three murders now. Why haven't they been picked up by now, Inspector?"

"Because in spite of putting the appeal in the media, people have been slow in coming forward with a possible name for the culprit. We can only go on the evidence or clues presented to us, and at present, they're disappointingly minimal." She had no intention of telling him they had possibly discovered the offender's bike.

"What is wrong with people? Someone must know the individual who has done this, or could it be possible that more than one person is involved? Have you thought about that, Inspector?"

"Yes, we've thought about that. However, with the witness statements we have to hand, we believe we're only looking for the one offender. Right, we better get on with the investigation. Ring me if Brenda's name comes to mind in the next day or so."

Dave and Kayli followed Lincoln back to the bar area, where Kayli shook Lincoln's hand.

After they'd left the bar, Dave asked, "Do you think he was genuine?"

Kayli opened the car door and slipped inside before she replied. "He seemed genuine enough. Maybe we should call back to Brenda's husband to pick up a photo. I should have asked you to pick one up. Did you ask the husband where Brenda worked?"

Dave grimaced. "Sorry, I forgot about that. I'm so used to you dealing with the victims' families in instances like this that it completely slipped my mind when the husband got upset. He was sobbing. I hadn't anticipated that."

Kayli smiled. "No problem. I know you were out of your comfort zone. It's a tough part of the job, right?"

"You're not kidding. I'm sure he won't mind if we drop back."

"That's what we'll do then."

~ ~ ~

Kayli halted the car outside the large semi-detached property in the quiet cul-de-sac and spotted a man tending to the late-blossoming roses in his front garden. "Is that Mr. Godfrey?"

"Yeah, that's him. Strange that he's out here, gardening, considering the news I delivered only a few hours ago."

"People deal with their grief in different ways. You know that, Dave. Are you coming, or would you rather stay here?"

"Never been given the option before, boss. I'll stay here and let you deal with him."

Kayli left the keys in the ignition and exited the car. She walked up the path towards the man, her warrant card at the ready. "Hello, Mr. Godfrey. My name is DI Kayli Bright."

The man peered at her ID and nodded. "One of your lot has already been here to tell me about my wife," he said, his eyes brimming with tears. "I couldn't sit inside the house a moment longer. The walls were closing in on me. Thought I'd do a spot of gardening instead. The roses were Brenda's favourites."

"I'm so sorry for your loss, Mr. Godfrey. My partner broke the news to you earlier whilst I attended another scene. Unfortunately, he forgot to ask where your wife was employed."

He snipped at a dead rose head and watched it tumble to the ground. "She was a receptionist at the doctor's down the road. Been there for almost thirty years, give or take. She had a few years off to bring up the children but returned once they went to school."

"I see. Can you tell me the name of the surgery?"

"Yes, Churchwoods. May I ask why you need that information?"

"Just for our enquiries. Maybe your wife had been having problems at work with someone. Is that possible, sir?"

He shook his head, and his mouth turned down at the sides. "No. Definitely not. She would have told me. My wife and I never kept secrets from each other, Inspector." Tears dripped on to his cheeks. "Damn, I miss her already. Why did this have to happen to her?"

"Why don't we go inside, and I'll make you a nice cup of tea?" She hooked her arm through his and pushed open the front door. The man slipped off his tatty gardening shoes, placed them behind the door, and pointed the way to the kitchen. Kayli went ahead of him. The house was nicely decorated, and she could tell instantly that it was owned by an older generation by the little knickknacks on the hall table and the faded floral paintings on the walls in the hallway.

The kitchen units were also dated, but the room itself was very clean and tidy. Kayli filled the kettle and watched as the man sat down at the table and buried his head in his hands.

"I don't know how I'm going to cope without Brenda. She was my world. We used to sit here every day and just laugh together. I can hear her laughter all around me now ... Do you think her spirit is here with me?"

Kayli smiled at the weary-looking gentleman. "I've heard of it happening. I've never experienced it myself, though, sir." She looked over at a dresser along one wall and crossed the room to take a closer look at a picture of the husband and wife holding hands on a beach. "She looked a kindly soul."

"Never said a bad word about anyone. Everyone loved her. I know you'll think me silly, but I haven't broken the news to our children yet. I'm too scared to. I don't know how to tell them that they'll never see her again. I know I should have told them by now ... I just can't find the right words."

"It is difficult, Mr. Godfrey. Would you rather I did it for you?"

His eyes widened. "Would you?" Then his head dropped onto his chest. "No, perhaps not. I should do it myself. It wouldn't be right to hear it from a stranger ... no offence, dear."

"None taken. Maybe you should ask them to call round here to see you. Do they visit much?"

"Yes, I'm lucky in that respect. Both children live close by, and we see each other weekly. That's where Brenda was last night, in fact—at Sandra's house, looking after the children while she and her husband celebrated their anniversary. If only she'd stayed the night there, she wouldn't have been on the road at that ungodly hour, and she'd still be al ... here today."

"That is very sad. Maybe I could ring your children for you and ask them to come round now, while I'm here. Would that be possible?"

"I'd appreciate that. Sandra will be at home with the little ones, and my son, Matt, will be at work. He's a local delivery driver, so it shouldn't be too difficult for him to drop by. I'll get you their numbers."

"I'll make the drink and then ring them. Is it all right if I make one for myself while I'm at it?"

"Of course." He reached for his mobile in the centre of the kitchen table and flipped through the phone. He jotted down the numbers on a nearby notebook and handed the sheet of paper to Kayli when she placed the mugs of tea on the table.

Swallowing, she dialled the first number. "Hello, is this Sandra?"

"Yes," a woman replied hesitantly.

"Hello, Sandra, you don't know me, but I'm at your father's house at the moment. Is there any chance you can drop by and see him?"

"You're not making sense. Is Dad all right? Who are you?"

"Sorry, I'm DI Bright of the Avon and Somerset Constabulary. I'd rather not say more over the phone."

"Oh my God. You can't leave me up in the air like that. What's going on?"

"Please, I'd rather tell you in person. It's nothing to worry about," she added, sensing the fear in the woman's voice.

"The police turn up at my father's house, and you tell me it's nothing to worry about! Are you crazy?"

"I'm sorry. Please, if you could come over as soon as possible, I'd appreciate it."

"I'm on my way. Let me gather the children together. I should be with you in fifteen minutes, max."

"Thank you. We'll see you soon." Kayli hung up and smiled at Mr. Godfrey. "I can understand why you found it difficult now. I hope your son will be less inquisitive."

"I doubt it. Good luck, Inspector."

Kayli took a sip of tea and then placed the second call. "Hello, is this, Matt?"

"It is. Who is this? I'm driving at present. Can I call you back?"

"I'm DI Kayli Bright, sir. Is it possible for you to call at your father's address? I'm with him now."

"The police? Has Dad been arrested?"

"No, it's nothing to worry about. He'd like you and your sister to be here with him. That's all."

"Why? Oh God, has something happened to Mum? Is that what you're telling me?"

"How soon can you be here? Sandra is on her way," Kayli replied, sidestepping his question.

"I'm just dropping off a parcel locally. I should be free within a few minutes. I could be there in around twenty minutes."

"Thank you. We'll see you then." She hung up before he could ask any more awkward questions.

Mr. Godfrey reached across the table and patted her hand. "Thank you, dear."

"You're welcome. I sense that was the easy part. I'll be right back. I need to let my partner know what's going on." She rushed through the house and out to the car. Dave had his head back with his eyes closed. Kayli thumped on the window, and he almost hit the roof of the car.

"What the fuck ... you nearly gave me a heart attack. Everything all right?"

"His son and daughter are coming over. I wanted to let you know we could be here a while. Do you want to stay here or come inside?"

"I'll stay out here and catch up on some sleep, if it's all the same to you."

"Fine. I could be here for some time."

"Good luck. Don't envy you that task."

Kayli rolled her eyes and returned to the house, where she found Mr. Godfrey staring at the picture of his wife in the kitchen. "Would it be possible to get a picture of your wife, Mr. Godfrey? It'll help with our enquiries."

"Do you want this one?"

"It's up to you. Any will do."

His hands shaking, he removed the photo from the frame and slid it across the table to her. Kayli slipped it into her pocket as the back door opened and a young woman with two children entered.

CHAPTER THIRTEEN

An hour later, feeling emotionally wrecked, Kayli left the house. The Godfreys' children had pleaded with her to find the person responsible for their mother's murder, and she'd promised them it would be her top priority.

The drive back to the station was subdued. Kayli and Dave walked up the stairs to the incident room on heavy, weary legs. Donna and Graeme seemed equally weary when she and Dave entered the room. "Everything all right, guys?"

"Frustrated, boss. Not sure where to turn next," Graeme replied.

"Okay, why don't we try and trace the CCTV footage for around the river where the bike was found, Graeme? The culprit must have got away somehow. Was that on foot, or did they have a second vehicle waiting for them?"

Graeme sat forward in his chair. "Gotcha. I'll look into it now."

"Apart from that, our hands are tied until Forensics give us the results from the bike. They said that would likely come in at the end of the day. I'll chase it up at five if I haven't heard anything by then. Donna, please can you do a background check on a Brenda Godfrey? Not sure what it will likely turn up, if anything, but whatever you find will be a bonus. Can you also scan this photo of the victim for me?"

Donna took the photo and placed it in the copier beside her. "Where do you want me to send the file?"

"To my phone, if you would."

Within seconds, Kayli's phone registered that the image had come through. She rang Lincoln's number.

"Hello, Lincoln James."

"Hi, Lincoln. It's DI Bright. I'm just going to send you a photo of Brenda Godfrey. Can you take a look, see if you recognise her or not?"

"Will do. I'll ring you straight back."

Kayli hung up, downloaded the photo, then sent it in a message. Her phone rang a few seconds later.

"Yes, I know the face. I'm trying to place her now."

"Would it help if I told you where she worked?"

"It might do."

"Churchwoods doctor's surgery."

"That's it. Yes, that's my doctor. Crikey, that's a pretty loose connection to me, if that's where this is leading."

"It's a connection. That's all we need at this point. Thanks for that. I'll be in touch soon."

She hung up and crossed the room to the whiteboard. After picking up the marker pen, she added Brenda's name then wrote down the connection between all three victims. Dave joined her.

"That's bizarre, if that's the reason behind her death."

Kayli folded her arms and stared at the board. "You're not wrong. Nothing about this case should surprise us, though."

"It's still all pointing back to Lincoln. The question is: what are we going to do about that?"

"There's nothing we can do yet, Dave. Not without the identification of that bike. However, there is one thing in our favour."

"What's that?"

"The offender no longer has the vehicle to terrorise people with."

"Hmm ... he might not have that particular vehicle, but the odds are he'll have the use of another vehicle to hand. That alone could infuriate us even more. He could switch vehicles all the time from now on. That'll leave us up the creek and pulling our hair out if he explores that option."

"You're not wrong, partner."

A few hours later, at five on the dot, Kayli picked up the phone in her office and rang the forensic lab to chase up the results.

A technician answered the call right away and delivered some very discouraging news. "The machine we use to decipher objects that have been vandalised has broken down. We were halfway through the test when it malfunctioned."

"Damn, shit, and blast. Where do we go from here? I need those results ASAP."

"I'm aware of that, Inspector. I can only offer my succinct apologies. I've been onto the manufacturers, and they're going to do their best to either send an engineer out or, failing that, deliver a temporary machine over the weekend."

Kayli sighed heavily. *So frigging near and yet so far!* "What about using another machine in a different area? This can't be the only machine in circulation, surely?"

"It's costly equipment. What with the cutbacks everyone is suffering at present, I'm not sure how many labs are likely to have one of these babies."

"Can you try and ring them for me? It's vital we get those results soon."

"I can ring around. I'm not holding out much hope, though. I want you to be aware of that."

"All I can ask is that you do your best." She reeled off her mobile number. "Can you keep me informed over the weekend?"

"I'll get one of my colleagues to ring you. I'm going away for the weekend, sorry."

"Lucky you. All I'm trying to do is keep the streets of Bristol safe. I can't do that without the results of those tests."

"I understand. This will be treated as an urgent matter, I assure you."

"Thanks. Ring me the minute you know something." Kayli hung up and let out an exasperated scream.

Dave appeared in the doorway to see what the commotion was about. "Are you okay?"

"No. I need to get out of here. This place, or should I say this investigation, is driving me effing nuts."

"What's wrong?" he asked, puzzled.

"They're not going to be able to give us the results on the bike until well after the weekend. The damn machine has broken down."

"Jesus! That's a bummer. Is there nothing else they can try?"

"Apparently not. I asked them to try a different district for help, but there aren't many of these machines in circulation because of the cost implications. We're screwed, Dave."

"Hey, this isn't like you, Kayli, to be so defeatist. Go home. You've been here since four. There's nothing we can do until after the weekend anyway."

"You're right. Christ, Mark is due home, and I haven't done a thing around the house. I've not been home for a couple of days, and there is no food in the fridge, either."

"Hey, I doubt that's going to matter to him. He'll be dying to see you. Why don't you shoot off?"

"Thanks. I need to ensure uniform keep vigilant on their patrols over the weekend first."

"No, you don't. I can do that. Just go."

"I hate running out on you like this."

Dave laughed. "Your logic baffles me at times. You're not running out on me. Got that?"

She smiled, gathered her handbag, and rushed out of the office, planting a sneaky peck on his cheek as she passed. "You're a star. Have a good weekend. Let's hope Monday brings us a positive start to the week."

"Have a good one. Say hi to Mark for me."

She smiled at her partner. Hearing Mark's name made her stomach jittery. Why was she feeling nervous about seeing him again? It had only been two weeks since he left. She drove home on autopilot, then suddenly realising she'd pulled up outside her front door, she swallowed the bile that had risen in her throat.

Kayli hesitated before she exited her vehicle, glancing up at the bedroom window to see if Mark was looking out for her. He wasn't, but then she was earlier than usual anyway. Inhaling a deep breath, she locked her car and strode up the path as if everything were normal, despite the way her insides were coiling into a nervous knot.

Walking into the lounge, she found Mark sitting on the sofa with a can of beer in his hand. He had his head leaning back against the couch, and his eyes were closed. The room was silent. No music or TV on. That was most unusual for him, as he hated silence in the house. She tiptoed towards him and tried to remove the can from his hand. His eyes flew open. His gaze burned into hers until he realised who she was, then the familiar sparkle appeared. He grabbed her hand, yanked her onto his lap, and kissed her, long and hard, almost too hard. She slipped her arms around his neck, happy to set aside her fears for a few blistering moments of passion.

As she pulled away, her eyes were moist with tears. "God, I've missed you."

"Not half as much as I've missed you. You're early. I wasn't expecting you."

"Long day. I started at four this morning."

"What? They're taking the piss."

She smiled, not having the heart to tell him that she'd worked nineteen hours the day before. He would have gone ballistic if he knew that. "Part of the job, love. You know that. I have a serial killer on my patch and needs must at the moment. When did you get back?"

She studied his face. He was more tanned than when he'd left, not surprising considering the heat where he'd come from. "I got back about four. I was going to prepare dinner, but the fridge is empty."

Her head dipped, ashamed. "Sorry, I've been super busy, and I've spent the last two nights round at Annabelle's."

His head tilted. "How come?"

"She was missing Giles, and she's not been very well."

His eyes drifted the length of her body. "You've lost a lot of weight yourself. Is everything okay?"

She kissed him on the lips. "I'm fine. Even better now my man is back home. What about if we have a takeaway tonight, and I'll nip to the shops to replenish the cupboards and the fridge tomorrow?"

"Suits me. I might even be persuaded to come to the supermarket with you."

She touched his forehead with the back of her hand. "Are you feeling all right?"

"Cheeky. I know it's a rarity, but I want to spend all my time off with you. I have no intention of letting you out of my sight again, for the foreseeable future, anyway."

"While that's very sweet to hear, is there any reason for that?" It was a strange statement for him to announce. They had never had the type of relationship where they were in each other's pockets before, and she was unsure how she felt about it. Usually, although they enjoyed each other's company, they both had their own friends they liked to socialise with, not that she'd had much time to do that in the past couple of months due to the pressure of her workload.

"No reason, except that I've missed you and I intend showing you how much over the weekend. You have got the weekend off?"

"Yes, I've got the weekend off, unless a major crime happens and I get called in—you know what it's like."

"Let's keep our fingers crossed. What do you fancy for dinner?" he asked, his eyes glinting.

Kayli got off his lap, took his hand, and led him upstairs. "I think we'll have dessert first."

CHAPTER FOURTEEN

In spite of their desperate need to top up the cupboards with food, Kayli and Mark spent most of Saturday in bed. At five o'clock, Kayli finally announced they needed to get to the shops. Reluctantly, Mark agreed. They showered and changed before setting off for Morrison's a few miles away.

"Fancy a pizza for tonight? Or do you want me to cook a proper meal?" she asked, screwing her nose up at the thought. "Bearing in mind we're going to Mum and Dad's for a barbeque tomorrow. There will be enough salad and meat on offer to feed a small army if I know Mum."

"Pizza and a good movie will be fine by me. I'll get a few bottles of wine, and we'll be good to go." He kissed her on the cheek and marched towards the alcohol aisle.

Kayli swiftly made her way around the rest of the supermarket in record time without him constantly stopping to pop extra supplies in her trolley. She sought him out at the end of the beer aisle and shook her head. He was struggling to hold five bottles of wine and eight cans of beer in his arms. "Do you think you've got enough there? Actually, we can't show up to the barbeque empty-handed. Why don't you pick up a couple of boxes of wine, and we'll take those to my folks'?"

He dumped the items he was juggling into the trolley and walked back to the wine section to retrieve two boxes of wine, one red and one white.

"Okay, that's all. This lot is going to cost a fortune."

Mark grinned, stuck his hand in his back pocket, and pulled out his wallet. He handed it to her. "Take it out of there."

Kayli's eyes bulged when she saw the notes filed neatly within its folds. "Jesus, looks like a year's salary for me in there."

He shrugged. "I told you it was well paid."

"You did. What you neglected to tell me was how much." Her police brain kicked into action. *No normal security job pays this kind of money.* She was tempted to grill him about what his job entailed exactly but not in the middle of the supermarket—that was something she needed to do when they were in the privacy of their own home.

An hour later, with the groceries put away and the pizza cooking in the oven, that was what Kayli did. They were sitting at the kitchen table, drinking a cup of coffee, when she broached the subject.

"I know we don't usually discuss how much each of us earns, love, but seriously, you can't flash about a stuffed wallet like that and expect me to keep quiet."

His gaze dropped to the table, and he paused a long time before he responded. "It's well paid. That's all you need to know for now, love."

"How well paid? And what is it they expect you to do for the money?"

He turned his mug on the table, avoiding eye contact with her, raising her suspicions.

"Mark, you're beginning to worry me now. What's going on?" She reached for his hand, and he flinched beneath her touch. "Mark, speak to me."

He exhaled loudly. "Why all the questions? I'm not one of your suspects. You don't need to cross-examine me all the time, Kayli."

"I'm doing nothing of the sort. I'm merely asking what your job involves, love."

"Security. That's all you need to know. Some jobs demand higher recompense than others. It's just the way it works out there," he said, still avoiding her gaze.

Kayli's blood was beginning to boil. She hated being kept in the dark about things. "Jesus, Mark! Talk to me. What does your job involve?"

Refusing to look up, he shook his head. "Leave it, Kayli. The last thing I want to do is fall out with you over this. Most women would be grateful for the money I'm bringing home."

"Well, you should know me well enough by now that I'm not most women."

He stood up and glared at her. "Don't I know it. I'll be in the living room, watching TV."

"What the hell is that supposed to mean?" she called after him.

He refused to answer. Kayli stood up and looked out the back window at the overgrown lawn, determined not to shed the tears pricking at her eyes. *So much for having a fun-filled, stress-free weekend. I have a right to ask the question, don't I?*

The alarm on the oven buzzed, and she felt relieved that she'd set it. Otherwise, she feared she would be serving up burnt offerings, and that would have made Mark's mood a whole lot worse.

She divided the pizza into thirds and put two on Mark's plate. When she tried to hand him his plate, he refused to take it, so she left it on the table in front of him. She sat at the other end of the sofa and began nibbling on hers, not that she had any appetite left as her stomach was twisted into knots. She hated confrontations at home.

Mark's pizza was almost cold before he started eating it. Kayli took her half-eaten dinner into the kitchen and threw it in the bin. Then she poured herself a glass of wine and returned to the lounge.

"No wonder you're skinny, if that's all you eat," he mumbled, his gaze remaining on the TV screen.

Kayli knew there was no point responding to his snarky comment and sipped her wine instead.

They spent the rest of the evening in silence, watching dross on the TV. At nine o'clock, Kayli announced she was going to bed. Mark grunted a goodnight as she left the room. Exhausted from the pressures of her work, she descended into sleep before long. At three, she awoke to find Mark's side of the bed empty. Tears slipped down her cheeks. She hated falling out with him, but she had no intention of going downstairs to find out where he was and why he hadn't come to bed. Eventually, she dropped off to sleep again around five. She woke at eight to the sound of the shower running. She sat up in bed, waiting for him to come out of the bathroom.

He entered the bedroom, towelling his hair dry, a small towel draped around his waist. Again, he avoided any form of eye contact with her and neglected to even acknowledge her.

She coughed slightly. "Morning." He ignored her, so she tried again. "Mark, please don't ignore me. I said good morning."

His eyes narrowed when he looked at her. "Morning. Are you going to stay in bed all day?"

She closed her eyes and bit down hard on her tongue. Then she threw back the cover and walked into the bathroom for a shower. When she returned, the room was empty. She strained her ear to hear the kettle boiling in the kitchen. Kayli took her time drying her long hair and decided to leave it loose for the day. After peering out the window to see if the sun was shining, she removed a pretty floral dress from her wardrobe and slipped it over her head. Then she applied the lightest of makeup before going downstairs for round two with Mark. She hoped that the sun shining through the kitchen window had improved his mood.

He turned to look at her when she walked into the room. His eyes widened, and a smile touched his lips. "You look beautiful."

She twirled, excited by his words. Maybe they were in for a good day after all. "Why thank you, kind sir. You don't look so bad yourself."

He was wearing his best jeans and the expensive burgundy Ben Sherman shirt she'd bought him for Christmas. She walked towards him and raised her face, expecting a kiss. He pecked her on the cheek instead of the lips and turned to make a mug of coffee. He handed it to her and smiled.

"Look, I'm sorry for interrogating you last night. I have no right to ask how much you earn or what risks you're taking with your life."

"You're right. You don't. But I acted like a child, and I apologise for that. Can we draw a line under it for today and enjoy the barbeque?"

"I'm all for that. I can't wait to see Giles. Is he okay?"

"Yeah, he's the same as always. Eager to see Annabelle and Bobby."

Kayli smiled, thinking of the surprise announcement Annabelle intended to make at the barbeque. It was going to blow her brother's socks off. She pondered telling Mark but decided against it, wanting him to be as surprised as her brother. "She's missed him, and so has Bobby."

"Likewise. They were all he talked about while we were away."

"That's lovely to hear. They're so happy together."

"Is that a dig?" he asked.

At first, Kayli found it difficult to tell if he was joking or not until a smile tugged at his mouth. She slapped his upper arm. "I'm sorry."

"Enough already, we're past that. What time do you want to set off?"

"We'll have this and go if you like. I'm not going to bother with breakfast. I know what kind of spread Mum usually puts on."

"How much have you lost?"

She hitched up her shoulders. "Around half a stone. I haven't had much appetite since you've been away."

"You're going to have to get used to it, Kayli. There's talk of this job lasting for well over a year."

"What? You're having me on, right?"

He shook his head. "No. Just think of the money. You've seen what I can earn. This means we'll be able to have a decent wedding and upsize the house all within twelve months."

Kayli clenched and unclenched her fists, trying not to let her temper get out of hand. "I was talking to Annabelle the other night and think I want to go down the wedding abroad route, if that's all right with you?"

"You discussed it with Annabelle before running it past me?"

"You weren't here," she said, instantly regretting her words as the smile disappeared from his eyes. Kayli drank most of her coffee and left the table to rinse her mug under the tap.

Mark scraped his chair on the lino floor, and it tipped over in his haste to cross the room towards her. "Since when do you discuss our future plans with other people before running it past me first?" He was inches away from her, towering over her, his hot breath intimidating her.

In the exact situation involving a suspect, she would have had no hesitation in kneeing him in the balls, but this was the man she loved and intended to marry. "We had a conversation. That's all. I haven't booked anything. I had every intention of running it past you first. What's wrong with you? I haven't been able to say a thing right since you came home. I can do without this shit, Mark."

He relented, ran a hand through his short hair, and stepped back. "Sorry. I'm on edge for some reason. I've been working flat out for two weeks. After so much time unemployed, I guess it has come as a shock to the system."

"Apology accepted. Please try not to snap when we're at the barbeque this afternoon. People are bound to ask questions, and you're going to be expected to answer them without biting someone's head off."

"All right. I hear you, Kayli. No need to go on like an old fishwife."

Her mouth gaped open. He'd never spoken to her like that before in all the years they had been together. He'd changed so much in the past two weeks, and she wasn't sure she liked the character he'd become. On-the-job pressure or not, there was no way she was about to put up with such shit.

He turned to walk out of the room, and she heard the front door slam. *What the hell? Now he's walked out on me.* Kayli ran to the lounge window and saw him get in the car. Instead of starting the engine, he let his head fall forward onto the steering wheel. He looked a broken man. Her heart went out to him even though moments earlier she'd thought he was about to punch the living daylights out of her. She was confused by his actions. No matter what he was going through, he had no right to take his bad mood out on her.

She gathered her handbag and the carrier bag with the wine they'd purchased then locked the front door on her way out. Mark was still sitting in the same position when she opened the passenger door. She placed a hand on his forearm, and he jumped a mile. "Hey, what's going on?"

"Nothing. Let's just have some fun today," he replied, staring at the parked vehicle ahead of them.

"Let's go. Mum will be expecting me to help prepare the salads."

Saying nothing more, he pulled out of the parking space and drove to her parents' in silence. When they arrived, Kayli was relieved to see that Giles's car was parked in her parents' drive. If anyone could tell her what was going on with her man, he could.

Mark took the carrier bag from her and hooked her arm through his as they walked across the gravel to the front door. They waited for one of her parents to open the door to greet them. He leaned over and whispered, "I'm sorry. I do love you, Kayli."

His words brought unexpected tears to her eyes. "I love you too. You know that. It's why I care so much."

Her father opened the door. He looked well. His retirement from army life was obviously suiting him.

"Hello, Dad. How are you?"

"Can't complain, love. Your mother keeps me on my toes better than the army ever did." He chuckled before kissing her cheek. "Come in. Lovely to see you, Mark. Giles is through there with Annabelle and Bobby. Go out and join them."

"I'll nip and say hello and then pop in to help Mum with the salads."

"It's all under control, love. Your mother has been at it for hours."

Kayli tore through the house, shouting a quick hi to her mother as she flew past the kitchen and out the back door. She screeched when she saw Giles then ran at him. Jumping into his arms, the way she always did when she hadn't laid eyes on him in a while, she nearly knocked him off his feet. They had a strong sibling bond, which Kayli attributed to the fact that their mother had home-schooled them. "Giles. I've missed you so much." She kissed him several times over his face.

He placed her on the floor, laughing at her enthusiasm. "Wow, sis, anyone would think I've been away for two years instead of a paltry two weeks."

"Bloody hell. You got a better reception than I did," Mark complained.

Kayli turned sharply to look at him. He was smirking, and for a moment, he sounded serious. "That's crap, and you know it." She hugged her sister-in-law next. "Hi, Annabelle, how are you? Long time, no see." They both laughed.

"I'm fine now I've caught up on my sleep," Annabelle said with a mischievous wink.

"Oh yes, what have I missed?" Giles asked.

Kayli smiled. "Wouldn't you like to know?" She reached down and lifted Bobby into her arms, rubbed his cheek, and tried to kiss him, but the little tyke fidgeted to get away from her red-stained lips. "Aww ... go on, sweetie, let Auntie Kayli kiss you."

Her nephew squeezed his eyes tight and relaxed a little in her arms. She kissed his cheek hard, making sure she left a lipstick mark on his skin, and all the adults laughed as Bobby wriggled to be set free. Kayli set him down, hugged her brother again, then hooked arms with Annabelle and steered her into the house. "I think our presence is needed elsewhere."

Once they were out of earshot of the others, Kayli asked Annabelle, "Have you told him the good news yet?"

"Nope. I thought I'd announce it after we've eaten, not that I fancy much. He's noticed I've lost weight and that I look tired. Thankfully, I wasn't sick this morning."

"Ditto. That was the first words out of Mark's mouth when he saw me. Do they think we're not going to worry about them while they're away?"

"Probably. Hopefully, Giles won't be going away again once I break the news."

"I wish Mark didn't have to go back there. He says the money is fantastic but refused to tell me any details about the job, which only makes me more worried about him. We had a fight about it last night, and he spent the night on the sofa."

"Oh no. That's the last thing either of you wants. No job is worth falling out over, love."

"Yeah, my sentiments entirely. He seems in a brighter mood today. Surprised me by announcing he loved me as we were standing on the front doorstep."

"Aww ... of course he loves you. You can tell that by the way he looks at you, Kayli."

"I wonder sometimes, that's all."

"Hey, we all have doubts like that, even me. I haven't got a clue how Giles is going to react once I share the news. I'm debating whether to leave it until we get home and tell him privately."

"He worships the ground you walk on, love. He'll be fine—no, delighted by the announcement. I guarantee it."

They reached the kitchen just as Kayli's mother was instructing her father to start ferrying the meat into the garden.

"Hi, Mum, the troops have arrived."

Her mother offered her cheek for Kayli to kiss. "Hello, dear. My, what a pretty dress that is. You should wear your hair down more often. It really suits you."

Kayli felt her cheeks warm under her mother's admiring glance. "Thanks, Mum. Anything Annabelle and I can do?"

"I could have done with a hand a few hours ago. I think everything is ready to go now. Go on out into the garden and enjoy yourselves with the boys. Make the most of their time at home."

"If you're sure. What about the salad dressing? Have you made that yet?"

"Damn, I always forget to make that. Why you lot can't be satisfied with a squeeze of mayonnaise over your salads, I'll never know."

Kayli laughed. "We like both. We're uncouth, remember?"

"Lord knows where you picked that ghastly habit up from. It certainly wasn't from either your father or me. You know where all the ingredients are. I'll help your father take the food outside."

Kayli and Annabelle gathered all the ingredients and measured them very roughly into a glass bowl. It was up to Kayli to taste it as pouring the oil into the dressing made Annabelle feel a little queasy. "Do you want to go to the toilet before Giles sees how green you look?"

"I think I will. Make my excuses for me. I won't be long."

Giles looked beyond Kayli when she walked into the garden, carrying the bowl of dressing. "Don't look so worried. She hasn't run out on you. She's in the loo."

"I'm not worried ..." He bristled. "Just concerned."

The next hour or so consisted of them all eating far too much and downing too many glasses of wine, except Annabelle, who stuck to the orange juice, which didn't go unnoticed by her husband.

"I want to drive home today," she told him with a grin.

He narrowed his eyes, and Kayli wondered if he suspected she was pregnant.

A few minutes later, after their mother had served up the home-made strawberry cheesecake, Annabelle tapped the side of her glass with her spoon. "Can I have everyone's attention please?"

They all quietened down and looked her way. She blushed a little, and Kayli thought how nice it was to see some colour back in her cheeks for a change.

"I'd like you all to raise your glasses. We need to celebrate the safe return of Mark and Giles."

"Hear, hear," Kayli shouted, looking back at Annabelle to see if she was going to announce anything else. Her sister-in-law seemed to be struggling to form her words. Kayli went to stand beside her as the others drank from their glasses and continued their conversation. "Are you all right, love?"

"I'm scared. Unsure how he's going to react. Maybe I should tell him when we're on our own."

"He won't react badly. I know him. He adores you and Bobby, and he's going to cherish the new arrival, as well. Just announce it. I'm here to give you support ... we all are."

Annabelle took a couple of large breaths. "Okay, you win. Wish me luck."

"Luck. Not that you'll need it."

Annabelle called for everyone's attention again. "There's more, everyone. I'd just like to say how much we've missed Giles and Mark. You never realise how much someone means to you until they're out of your sight and unavailable to speak to for a couple of weeks. I'm sure Kayli won't mind me divulging how much we've both struggled since their departure. She's kept me going this week when times were particularly tough because of this little one." Annabelle rubbed her stomach as her gaze locked with Giles's.

It took a few moments for her words to sink in before Giles rushed towards her and hugged his wife. Annabelle cried with relief, and it wasn't long before everyone else had cuddled and kissed her, delighted by the news.

"Now I know why you're not drinking. How pregnant are we?" Giles asked, his hand resting on Annabelle's flat stomach.

"Enough to cause me morning sickness while you've been away. I'm eight weeks. Kayli has been a rock this week, despite her heavy workload."

"You should have rung me," Kayli's mum said, looking slightly put out.

"We only found out at the end of the week, Mum. I forced Annabelle to do a home pregnancy test, and she didn't have it confirmed by the doctor until Friday," Kayli explained, throwing an arm around her mother's shoulders. "Isn't it exciting?"

"Of course it is, dear." Her mother gasped, and everyone turned to look at her. "What about your job, Giles?"

Giles's gaze drifted from his mother to Annabelle then Mark. "I'll have to give it up. There's no way I can continue with the baby due."

Kayli's heart lifted for Annabelle's sake as well as her own. It would be great to have Giles around full time again. She turned to face Mark, who looked as though he'd been punched by a professional boxer. She walked towards him and tucked her arm through his. "Isn't it great news about the baby, hon?"

"Yes."

"Are you all right?"

"Not really. This could be disastrous for me and my team. Giles is a valued member of our team, one who has a lot of experience that we rely on. I'm pretty ticked off by the timing of this announcement. I'm hoping Giles will give us one last tour before he jacks it in."

"I'm not sure that's going to happen, Mark. I think he's already made his mind up that Annabelle and the baby come first."

Mark shrugged out of her grasp and stepped away from the cheerful group. He picked up a can of beer from the table and crossed the garden to gaze down at the koi carp swimming in the fish pond her father had proudly created. Kayli decided to leave him alone for a while and to remain with the others celebrating the good news. Although the thought of having children had never crossed her mind, she loved Bobby and knew that she would adore the new arrival.

It was always great to have children around, as long as she could hand them back to the parents at the end of the day.

"Is Mark all right, love?" her father asked, sneaking up beside her.

She smiled at him and shrugged. "I guess he will be, Dad. It can't be helped. Giles is needed here. Annabelle has been having a really tough time of it this week. Mark needs to understand that people have different priorities in this life."

"Are you two getting on all right, love? He seems to have changed. Seems different somehow. Not sure how, but nothing gets past this old general."

"I'm not sure, to be honest, Dad. I think it would be best to leave him alone to get used to the idea. He hasn't said much about the job since he returned."

"That's not uncommon, love. I didn't tell your mother about the ins and outs of my job during my army days. More because I didn't want to bore her. It's not always exciting times serving in the army."

"I know that, Dad, but it's not as if he and Giles are serving with a regiment nowadays, is it? This is totally different, isn't it? I want to know what the boys are involved in, and to me, it's all a little too secretive for my liking."

"Why don't you try and have a quiet word with Giles in that case if you're not getting any joy from Mark?"

"I'd hate Mark to think I was going behind his back."

Her father leaned in and whispered, "Nonsense. Do it discreetly, and he'll never know."

"Thanks, Dad. I'll try and have a word with him before we leave."

"Do it. The less time you spend worrying about Mark, the better. It's not as if you haven't got a demanding enough job of your own to worry about. And don't think your mother and I haven't noticed how much weight you've lost since we last saw you. No point trying to disguise it by wearing that beautiful floaty dress of yours. We can see it in your face, darling."

She gently nudged him in the ribs. "I'm fine, Dad. I promise. My appetite has been wayward in the last few weeks. That's all."

He raised his hands. "I'll keep my nose out of it. Just promise me you'll take care of yourself."

"You old softie, of course I will. Thanks for caring. I better see what's going on with Mark. Just hope he doesn't snap my head off."

"If he does, he'll have me to contend with."

"Thanks, Dad, but I'd rather fight my own relationship battles."

"I know."

Kayli filled her glass from a bottle of Chardonnay on the table and walked towards Mark. She placed a hand on his back, and he flinched beneath her touch. "Sorry, I didn't mean to scare you. Everything all right?"

"Fine, and you didn't scare me. Do you have to sneak up on people like that?"

"Sorry," she replied, surprised by his harsh tone. Immediately, she regretted seeking him out and glanced across the garden at the smiles on the faces of the rest of her family then back at her fiancé, who seemed more distant from her now than he'd ever been in their relationship. She remained by his side, silent, for the next five minutes. The silence was interrupted by Mark's mobile ringing. He answered it on the second ring.

"Yep ... damn ... okay, I'll be there ASAP. No, I doubt he'll be coming back with me ... I'll explain when I get there."

"Who was that, Mark?" Kayli asked, her heart pounding.

"The guy I work for. I need to get the first flight back out there."

Her mouth gaped open for a split second before she found her voice. "What? But you've only just got back."

"I'm well aware of that, Kayli. It's my job. I go where and when they want to send me, no questions asked."

"Well, I'm damn well asking them. Why? Why you?"

"It's my *job*!" he sneered at her, baring his gleaming-white teeth.

Kayli shrunk back from him. There was clearly no sense arguing with him. "You better go then."

"Thanks for giving me your approval," he snarled. He walked away from her, slapped Giles on the back, whispered something in his ear, and disappeared into the house. She heard the front door slam and her car start up in the drive. Kayli stood rooted to the spot, bewildered. *What the hell? Did I deserve to be spoken to like that?*

A few seconds later, Giles joined her. "Sis, are you all right?"

She shook her head in disbelief. "No. If you must know, it feels like I've just been hit by an express train. What's going on with him, Giles? He's been in a foul mood since his return. Refused point-blank to tell me what the job involves or if it's dangerous, and now this. Jesus, I need answers. Not only because I'm a detective, but because I love that man. Although I barely recognise him now. I deserve answers, Giles, and I'm relying on you to give them to me."

He shook his head. "It ain't going to happen, sis. We had to sign an official secret kind of form."

Her head jutted forward, and her eyes widened until they hurt. "You what? Is this some kind of frigging wind-up?"

"No, sis. I'm sorry. I wish I could tell you. Let's just say I'm glad I decided to give up the job."

She threw her arms out to the side. "Oh, fucking great! That's reassured me no end, Giles. What am I supposed to think or say to that?"

"It is what it is, love. He loves you, and that's all you need to know."

"Does he? Words are cheap, aren't they? It's actions that really show someone how much they're loved, isn't it?"

"You're blowing this up out of all proportion, Kayli."

"You think?" she shouted. She looked over at the rest of the family, who were all frowning, looking concerned.

Her father joined them. "What's this all about, you two?"

"It's Kayli overreacting, Dad. That's all."

She couldn't hold her temper in any longer. She aimed a fist at her brother's arm and thumped him hard. "How dare you make this out to be all my fault! How bloody dare you, Giles?"

"See, there you go again."

Her father placed a comforting arm around Kayli's shoulder. "Calm down, love. Why don't we discuss this inside, in my office?"

"Because there's nothing to discuss, Dad. Mark has gone back out to Afghanistan, and neither he nor my darling brother here is willing to share why."

Her father glared at Giles. "Then I can understand why your sister is so upset. She deserves to know, Giles. Why has he gone back so soon? He's barely set foot in the door for five minutes. Granted, he's only been away two weeks on duty, but even so, why send him back home if they knew he'd be called upon in less than forty-eight hours? I'm with Kayli on this one, son."

Giles sighed heavily. "We had to sign a secrecy document, Dad. You know how that goes. I can't tell you what goes on out there."

Kayli growled and stormed into the house. She locked herself in the downstairs toilet and cried until her tear ducts dried up.

A gentle knock on the door startled her. "Sis, open the door."

"Leave me alone to wallow."

"I will not. Open this door, or I'll break it down, and you know I'm not joking."

She swiped the tears from her cheeks and pulled back the lock.

Giles yanked open the door then stepped into the confined space and gathered her in his arms. "Come on, Kayli. This isn't like you."

"I know it isn't. That's why I feel so ashamed. Why? Why has Mark refused to open up to me? He says he loves me, but surely, if he did, he would confide in me."

"He does love you. It's this damn secrecy paper we signed, love. It's nothing personal, I swear."

She buried her head in his shoulder as fresh tears welled up. He caressed the back of her head with one hand while the other clung to the small of her back. "I want the man I fell in love with back. I don't like the man he's become ... he's changed."

"Some men do that. He has a tough job now. He has to consider all the lives of the men serving under him, and it's a huge responsibility that is obviously taking its toll on him mentally."

"Then why couldn't he tell me that himself? Why pretend everything is all right when it clearly isn't?"

"I don't know, except that people deal with things differently when they're put in charge and the onus lies on their shoulders."

"You never had a problem with handling the responsibility when you were in charge."

"I know. He'll get better at separating his feelings once he becomes more accustomed to the role. Give him time, eh?"

She shook her head. "I'm not sure I can, Giles. My job is stressful enough without my personal life coming under attack every five minutes. Everyone deserves to be happy, don't they? I know I do, and look at me, bawling my eyes out because my fiancé walked out on me at a celebratory barbeque that has been especially laid on for the two of you. How is that right?"

Giles pushed her away from him. "Kayli, you're at it again. Overanalysing things and making them seem bigger than they are."

Furious, she tore herself out of his grasp. "If that's what you think, then maybe I should leave you all to your celebration and take my self-pitying notions and go home." She turned and stormed through the house to find her handbag. It wasn't until she reached the front door that she realised she had no means of getting home. So she set off on foot, without saying farewell to her parents.

She heard footsteps crunching on the gravel behind her and the clunk of central locking. "Get in the damn car. I'll take you home," Giles shouted.

"No, thanks. The walk will do me good. According to you, I need to get a lot of derisory thoughts out of my head anyway."

Giles groaned. "You know what, Kayli? You can be a real stubborn bitch at times. Do what you want. I'll make your apologies to Mum and Dad. They're going to be really hurt that both of you left without having the decency to say goodbye."

Kayli stopped dead. He was right. She was behaving totally out of character. *I will not let Mark change my personality with his selfish behaviour.* She spun around to face her brother, who was standing by his car door. "Anyone ever tell you that you can be a right bastard at times?"

"Not lately." He grinned, pressing the key fob to lock the car. He then held out his hand for her to take.

Slowly, feeling ashamed of her mini temper tantrum, she slipped her hand into his. "I'm sorry for behaving like a spoilt brat."

"You're forgiven. Stay strong, Kayli. He loves you, but maybe he's simply forgotten how to show you how much you mean to him."

"Maybe. I'll stay another half an hour then leave. No need for you to watch what you drink, though. I'll call a taxi to pick me up."

"Good. I was hoping you'd say that."

She dug him playfully in the ribs and sighed. "Why does life have to be so hard at times?"

"No idea. But let this be a lesson to you, Kayli. Remember we're always here for you, through the good times and the bad. You hear me?"

She leaned over and kissed his cheek. "Thanks, Giles. It means a lot to hear you say that. Great news about the baby. I'm glad you've decided not to go back out there with Mark, because Annabelle needs you here with her. This pregnancy has already taken its toll on her."

"I can tell. I had no hesitation. My family always comes first— you know that."

"Which is why I love you so much. You truly are one in a million, Giles. What will you do about work now?"

"Well, I got paid a fair whack for the past two weeks. If we're careful, that should see us through the next few months."

"Mind if I ask how much you got paid?"

"Ten grand."

She halted mid-step and turned to face him. "What?"

He shrugged. "I take it Mark didn't tell you that. Odds are that he picked up more than me, what with him being in charge of the team."

She shook her head. Her sudden willingness to return to the barbeque deserted her once more. "That's appalling. I can't ... I'm sorry ... Make my excuses to everyone. I have to get out of here."

She sprinted across the gravel and out of the drive before Giles could stop her. An hour later, she walked through the front door of her house. The home she and Mark had created together suddenly felt like a cell to her, imprisoning her in a morbid cocoon. She immediately went to the fridge and retrieved a bottle of white wine. She poured a glass and downed it in one gulp. She refilled her glass and went back into the lounge, where she spotted the note on the coffee table. One word was written in large capitals: SORRY!

CHAPTER FIFTEEN

Kayli felt like death warmed up the following morning. She'd set the alarm thirty minutes earlier than usual. After a cool shower, she dried her long hair and got ready for work, determined to not let Mark enter her mind. She'd given herself a good talking-to whilst consoling herself over the bottle of wine the previous evening. If he wanted to live his life in danger mode, then so be it. She refused to let his actions mess with her head or rule her life. From now on, she would think for herself and be more positive, not dwell on what he was doing thousands of miles away. Everyone around her was right—she had lost too much weight recently. *And for what? Worrying about a man who's so wrapped up in himself that my feelings don't matter.*

Screw that. I'm my own person. A successful woman in my own right. I don't need a man in my life to know that I can succeed. What am I saying? That it's over between Mark and me? The question repeated in her head over and over during her journey into work.

She was surprised to see the rest of the team already at their desks when she arrived. "Am I late?"

"Nope ... you're never late. We just agreed to come in early and go over things. A new week and all that," Dave replied, making his way over to the vending machine. He returned and placed a cup on the desk nearest to her.

"Gosh, and you're feeling generous too. Are you sure I haven't walked into the wrong office?"

His eyes narrowed. "And you wonder why I never go out of my way to do something nice for you!"

"It's appreciated. I've had a shocker of a weekend, but I'd rather not talk about that. The one positive I can take from this weekend is that it has made me determined to catch the bastard doing these crimes. Let me check the post, see if there's anything worth dealing with, and I'll be with you in five minutes. I take it we haven't had the results from the bike yet?"

"Nope. I chased Forensics as soon as I came in. The engineer is due around mid-morning, and they're hoping to give us the results sometime this afternoon."

"Excellent. Not long to wait now then." She ventured into her office, saw the stack of brown envelopes sitting on her desk, and left the room again. "On second thoughts, let's go over what we have so far."

The team gathered around, and Kayli stood alongside the white-board to recap where the investigation was at that point. "Loose ends, what do we have?"

"CCTV footage from the river where the bike was dumped?" Dave said, crossing his arms across his inflated chest.

"I'll get on that first thing, boss," Graeme assured her.

"Right, what else?" Kayli asked, her own mind not warming up as quickly as she'd hoped. Maybe that was due to the drink she'd consumed the day before.

"Didn't you say you wanted to visit Brenda Godfrey's place of work?"

Kayli pointed at her partner. "You're right. We'll finish up here and shoot over there first thing, Dave. Anything else?"

"I've checked the report for all the crimes that have taken place over the weekend, boss, and you'll be pleased to know I found nothing appertaining to our cases."

"That's a relief ... or is it? If the killer has dumped his bike, does this mean he's gone underground? Or rethought his actions and felt Brenda Godfrey's murder was a step too far?"

"I doubt it's the latter notion," Dave replied.

Kayli nodded. "I agree. Give me ten minutes to drink this, Dave."

"Sure, that means I've got time for another cup too."

Kayli bit the bullet and returned to her office to rip open her post. Her first instinct to leave it proved to have been the best plan of action. The envelopes contained nothing worth knowing. Certain procedures had changed, but the head office had written to her about them several times already. Another letter was chasing up a report about a past investigation that they'd been pestering her about for weeks. She groaned. "Okay, I better deal with that request when I get back, before they pull me over hot coals for being shoddy."

~ ~ ~

Around twenty minutes later, Kayli and Dave walked through the front door of Churchwoods doctor's surgery, where an older woman was on reception. The smell of old files tickled Kayli's nose, and she saw that the receptionist appeared to be having a clear-out of sorts.

"Is there a practice manager I can speak to?" Kayli asked.

"She's in with the doctors at present. They have a general meeting every morning before surgery begins. If you take a seat, she shouldn't be long."

"Thanks, we'll do that."

Kayli and Dave paced the area until another woman, who was in her late fifties to early sixties, joined the receptionist behind the desk. The receptionist pointed in their direction, and the other woman crossed the waiting room towards them.

"You wanted to see me? I'm the practice manager, Maureen Pitt."

"Yes, I'm not sure if you're aware, but in the early hours of Friday morning, Brenda Godfrey lost her life in a fatal incident."

The woman nodded. "We were told by her husband on Friday afternoon. It was a dreadful shock to us all. She was well loved here, not only by the doctors and other receptionists, but by the patients, as well. She'll be sorely missed. Of course, if there is anything I can do to help with the investigation, please feel free to ask."

"I'm not sure there is after that statement. I was wondering if Brenda had recently had any problems at work. Maybe she'd fallen out with a patient, and perhaps they'd taken umbrage with her over something work related?"

"No, nothing. She was one of the milder tempered amongst us. Nothing fazed her at all. She treated everyone as her equal, from the doctors to the patients."

"I see. Well, there's nothing else to ask, in that case." Over the woman's shoulder, a young blonde had joined the receptionist. Her gaze locked with Kayli's for a second or two before she turned away and disappeared behind the shelves of patient notes. Kayli had the feeling she'd seen the young woman before, but had trouble placing her.

"I'm sorry I couldn't help you. I hope you find the person responsible for this heinous crime. Brenda didn't deserve to go out that way. No one does."

"We're closing in on that person. Thanks for your help."

Kayli and Dave walked out the front door. Kayli stood on the doorstep, her mind working through a Rolodex of images as she sought out the answer to where she'd seen the girl on reception before.

"What's wrong?"

"Did you see her?" Kayli asked, her eyes scanning the car park.

"Who are you talking about?" Dave replied, shaking his head in confusion.

"The girl behind the reception desk, not the original woman we spoke to, the other one."

"I didn't notice her."

"Your powers of observation have always been your downfall, partner." All of a sudden, something slotted into place. "My God, I know her now! She was the girl sitting at the bar talking to Lincoln the first and second time we called in to see him at the bar. "I want a word with her." She pulled open the door and approached the receptionist again. "Sorry to trouble you. The young woman you were speaking to just a minute ago, where is she?"

"Melinda? She went to the toilet."

Kayli's heart raced. "Where is it?"

"Why?" the receptionist asked, a baffled expression settling on her face.

"Just tell me, please. We're wasting time."

The receptionist stood up and pointed at a set of double doors leading into the surgeries. "Through there, on the right."

"Thanks. Dave, with me."

They rushed through the doors and found the toilet with a silhouette of a female on the wall. "Stay here," she ordered. Sensing something was wrong, Kayli immediately dropped to the floor to look under the cubicle doors, but all the cubicles were empty. Jumping to her feet, she yanked open the door, spun a perplexed Dave around, and pushed him ahead of her. "She's not there. Quick, before she gets away, Dave." He bolted through the double doors, passed through the reception area and out to the car park, with Kayli hot on his heels. An old Ford Anglia was just about to leave the exit. "Stop her, Dave."

He leapt over the knee-high stone wall and caught up with the vehicle in the main road, but instead of stopping the car, the woman slammed her foot down on the accelerator and hurtled towards Dave.

"Stop!" Dave shouted his hand raised in front of him.

The car picked up speed, and Kayli shouted to her partner, "Get out of the way, Dave! She's not going to stop."

Dave stood his ground, and moments later, Kayli saw him catapult into the air and heard him cry out. *My God, she's probably killed him.* She ran back inside the surgery. "Get a doctor out front right away and call an ambulance." She then sprinted back out and across the car park to her partner to inspect the damage. Though she tried to run faster, fear made her muscles grow taut. "Dave! Dave, I'm here. Are you all right?"

He groaned. She lowered her head to try to hear what he was saying, but his words were indecipherable.

A young man with a medical bag knelt down beside her. "What happened?"

"Your receptionist mowed him down. Please help him," Kayli pleaded.

"What? You must be mistaken. None of our receptionists would do such a thing."

"I'm not going to argue the toss with you, Doctor. Just do what you can to help him." Hearing a siren in the distance, Kayli breathed a sigh of relief. Seconds later, the ambulance drew up beside them, and two paramedics joined them.

"Step back, miss. We'll handle it from here," the female paramedic assured her.

The second paramedic pulled Kayli gently to her feet. "He'll be fine."

"Will he? Please save him—he can't die," she pleaded to anyone prepared to listen to her.

The doctor stood aside after he'd apprised the paramedic of Dave's condition.

Shaking her head to clear her thoughts, Kayli removed her phone from her pocket and dialled the station.

Donna answered her call. "Boss? Are you okay?"

"I am, but Dave's been run over. They're taking him to hospital now. Jesus, one of the receptionists did this, Donna."

"Shit! Why?"

"She was running from us. I think she's the killer."

"Crap. Have you got a name for me to check, boss?"

"No—shit! Yes. Damn, all I've got is Melinda. Hang on a second, Donna." She scanned the area. "Doctor, what's Melinda's surname?"

"It's Walton," the doctor replied, his brow furrowed in puzzlement. "I'm sure this was an accident. She wouldn't have deliberately run your partner over."

"Wanna bet? She did! I saw it with my own eyes." She tutted and held her phone to her ear again. "Donna, get a bulletin circulated. Melinda Walton is driving an old light-blue Ford Anglia. There can't be many of those on the road. I want her found immediately. Get control on the case right away."

"I will, boss. I'll do the background checks on her and try and source her address for the patrol vehicles. Should they pick her up if they find her?"

"Yes, but tell them to be careful. She'll probably be armed and dangerous. I could run back into the surgery to get her address, but for all we know, she's given them a false one anyway, plus I want to stay with Dave. I'll be at the hospital until I know Dave is going to be okay. As it stands, it's touch and go. Crap! Can you call Suranne for me, make her aware of the situation, Donna? She'll want to be with him. I don't think I could tell her without breaking down. He's a mess. Poor Dave. He was only doing his frigging job."

"Stay positive, boss. That's all we can do for now."

"I'll try. Good luck. Let's get this bitch ASAP, Donna."

As Kayli ended the call, the paramedics were loading Dave into the back of the ambulance. "I'll follow you, if that's okay?"

"Of course. We'll be taking it easy, but he's pretty stable now."

Kayli heaved a relieved sigh. "Thank God for that." She turned to the doctor, who looked bewildered still. "Thank you for your assistance, Doctor."

"You're welcome. Not that I did much. I hope he's up and about soon."

"Thanks, so do I." Kayli raced back to her car and started the engine. She drew up behind the ambulance as it was pulling away.

CHAPTER SIXTEEN

An agonisingly slow ten minutes passed before they arrived at the A&E Department. She parked on a grass verge, not concerned if the hospital parking attendant was officious or not. She needed to stay with Dave every step of the way. The paramedics wheeled her unconscious partner through the short corridor into triage, where a nurse held up her hand, blocking Kayli's admittance.

"Sorry, you can't come in. Why don't you wait in the family room? A doctor will be along to see you once your friend has been assessed." She pointed down the corridor behind Kayli.

"Thank you. Please take care of him."

"Guaranteed." The nurse smiled and went through the doors, leaving Kayli feeling lost and alone. Her chin dropped, and she walked towards the family room, where she sat down in the nearest chair and buried her head in her hands. A few moments later, a familiar voice sounded beside her.

"Kayli ... he's not ... dead, is he?"

Her head shot up, and wiping the tears from her cheeks, she shot out of the chair. "Hello, Suranne, thanks for coming. No, he's not dead. The last I heard, he was stable."

They hugged, clinging to each other like long-lost family members who'd been reunited after twenty years apart. They parted and sat down.

"I had to come. Mum is looking after Luke. Donna said he was in a traffic accident. How did it happen?"

"We were chasing a suspect. Dave stood in front of the suspect's car to prevent her from leaving the scene, and she put her foot on the floor, drove right at him."

"Intentionally? You say the driver was a she? How could anyone —let alone a woman—do that?"

"It's beyond me, love. I shouted for Dave to get out of the way. No doubt he intended to at the very last moment, but the woman put her foot down and aimed at him. It was terrible to watch."

"I bet. What injuries has he sustained? Any idea?"

"Not sure. I think at least a broken leg. It was bloody and at an odd angle. The paramedics were brilliant, on the scene within minutes. There was no delay getting him here."

"That's a good thing, I think. Christ, I just can't believe that a woman could do this. A suspect you say?"

"Yes. Dave's told you about the cases we've been working on recently, yes?"

Suranne nodded.

"Let's just say that Dave got off lightly compared to her other victims."

"Crikey, the murderer ran him down." Suranne shook her head.

They sat in silence, grasping each other's hands, until the doctor entered the room. Kayli introduced herself and Suranne to the young male doctor, who had a kind-looking face.

"Here's where we stand. Mr. Chaplin has a broken leg, and we suspect a couple of broken ribs. We're going to send him down to X-Ray to confirm that, plus we'll need to do an MRI, then he'll be going straight into surgery. He's stable for now, but we need to act fast. There's no telling if he's suffered any internal bleeding during the accident."

"What are his chances, Doctor?" Kayli asked.

"Right now, I'd say they are fifty-fifty. It depends what the surgeon finds when he opens him up. I need to get back now. I'll keep you up to date as and when I can."

"Thank you," Kayli and Suranne replied in unison.

The doctor left the room, and they hugged each other again. Kayli was determined not to think negatively about her partner's chances.

After an hour, Kayli's patience was wearing thin, and she began to pace the floor in the family room.

Suranne sighed. "Kayli, why don't you go? I'll stay here. I'm sure you're chomping at the bit to get out there and find this woman."

Kayli smiled. "I am. I'm torn. I also want to stay here with you, to hear any news first-hand."

"I'll ring you as soon as I hear. Go. I would rather you were out there tracking this woman before she can harm anyone else."

Kayli reached for Suranne's hand. "Only if you're sure. I can be back here within half an hour, all being well."

"I insist. That's how Dave would want it. I'm certain of that."

Kayli hugged her, kissed her on the cheek, and rushed out of the hospital. Back in the car, she placed a call to Donna using the hands-free function. "Donna, I'm on my way back to base. Any news?"

"Yes, boss. I didn't want to disturb you until I was sure, but we think we've located the car."

"That's brilliant news. At the woman's address?"

"No, that's the thing. The woman held up another car and has swapped vehicles."

"Shit! Do we have eyes on her?"

"Graeme's tracking her on the cameras, and we're relaying the information to the patrol cars. They're not far behind her, boss."

"Excellent news. What area? I want to be there when they arrest the bitch."

"Going out towards St. Agnes on the Ashley Road."

"I'm on my way. Keep me informed. Is there a patrol vehicle at her address in case she turns up there?"

"Yes, there are two. One either end of her road, boss. I've also instructed a SOCO unit to pick up the vehicle and take it in for inspection."

"Well done, Donna."

"Boss, what's the news on Dave?"

"He's still in surgery. Not sure how long that's going to take. Suranne ordered me to leave and track down this woman. She'll ring me if there's any further news. It's fifty-fifty for now, Donna. Let's keep this positive momentum going. Dave wouldn't want us to be distracted by what's happening to him."

"Agreed. He'd be urging us to arrest this woman. I'll let you know as soon as I hear anything regarding her location, boss."

Kayli pressed the disconnect button on her steering wheel to end the call. *Focus, girl. No thinking about Dave—or Mark, for that matter. Concentrate on bringing this bitch in and punishing her for what she's done.* Suddenly realising her location, Kayli took the next left and pulled up outside Lincoln James's bar. She raced into the building.

Lincoln looked up at her, a mixture of fear and puzzlement dancing across his features. "Hello, Inspector. What can I do for you?"

She rushed toward the bar, reached over, and grabbed the front of his T-shirt. She hauled him to meet her. "Who is she to you?"

"Who? I haven't got a clue what you're talking about."

"The blonde you were having a drink with at the end of the bar the other day when we came in. Who is she?" She sneered as she spoke. She had been pushed too far over the last few days, and someone had to suffer.

He scratched his head. Kayli grabbed him again, tighter, ensuring that if he had any hairs on his puny chest, she caught some of them in her grasp.

"Ouch, you're hurting me. I think you're referring to Melinda. I can't be sure, though. Do you have a photo?"

"Stop wasting my time. You know damn well I'm talking about Melinda Walton. Who is she to you? No bullshit, James. I'm warning you—you're teetering on the edge of me hauling your arse in to charge you. So spill."

He tried to step back out of her grasp, but she held firm. "All right. I'll tell you if you loosen your grip."

Kayli unfurled her fingers slightly. "I'm waiting."

He heaved out a breath that swept over her face. "She's my girlfriend."

"She's *what*?"

"My girlfriend. We've been seeing each other for the past three months."

"But you were living with Carmen. You sick shit! Do you know what damage you've caused?"

"I have no idea what you're going on about. Melinda and I are going to be together now ..."

"Now that Carmen is out of the way? Is that it?"

He gulped, and his gaze dropped to the bar. "It wasn't planned. It just happened."

"Look at me, dickhead. You're frigging unbelievable. Whose idea was it to kill Carmen? Yours or hers?"

He shook his head, and his eyes widened in fear. "What? What are you talking about? Carmen had an accident, an unfortunate accident."

"You're bloody naïve if you think that, James. We've been investigating her murder from day one, and you *knew* that!"

"I thought it was an accident you were investigating. I can't believe what you're telling me."

"Utter bullshit!"

His gaze drifted around the bar when Kayli raised her voice. Everyone was staring in their direction, murmuring to the person standing next to them. "Can't we do this in my office?"

"I've got a better idea. Why don't we do this back at the station instead?"

"What? I haven't done anything wrong."

"Accessory to murder, for a start. You're coming with me." Still gripping the front of his T-shirt, she climbed onto the bar with the aid of the stool next to her and landed on the other side. She unhooked her cuffs from the back of her trousers and slapped them on his wrists before he had time to react.

"You're making a big mistake."

"We'll see about that." She held her thumb and forefinger in front of his face. "We're this close to capturing your bitch of a girl-friend. You'll both be behind bars, where you belong, before the day is out." She turned to face their audience. "The show is over, folks."

She pushed him along the length of the bar. "I'm innocent, I tell you. Completely innocent. You're making a big mistake. My solicitor will kick you off the force for this."

"Whatever. The satisfaction I'm feeling right now isn't about to be undone by your worthless lies or threats. You disgust me."

Kayli lifted his arms higher up his back, making it difficult for him to contemplate running or trying to escape. Once they were out of the pub, she placed him in the back of the car and jumped behind the steering wheel. She knew how risky it was taking him in by herself, but she had to get Melinda, and Lincoln was her only link. To get to the station faster, she flipped on her siren.

At the station, she tore Lincoln James from the vehicle and pushed him through the entrance to the station. "Sergeant Donaldson, put this man in a cell until I'm ready to question him later."

The sergeant rushed around the counter to collect the suspect. As soon as he was safely in the sergeant's hands, Kayli bolted out to the car again and continued on her journey out to St. Agnes. En route, she rang Donna to make her aware of the situation with Lincoln James.

"Excellent news, boss. I'm hearing that they've cornered Walton. I've instructed an ART to join our lads in case she has the shotgun with her."

"Brilliant. Are there Taser-trained officers at the scene, just in case?"

"Yes, I made sure there were. Everything seems to be falling into place, ma'am."

"Let's not count our chickens just yet, Donna. I'm five minutes away. What road should I be looking for?"

"They have her pinned down in Archer's Way. The ART is ten minutes away."

"I'll probably arrive at the same time they do."

"Good luck, boss. Be careful."

"Of course. See you soon," Kayli replied confidently. She ended the call and pushed her foot down on the accelerator.

She arrived at the scene to find four patrol cars already there. One had deliberately crashed into the passenger side of a white BMW, and the others had surrounded the vehicle so there was no way Melinda Walton could escape. She was sitting in the driver's seat, her head resting on the steering wheel. If anything, she looked defeated. However, Kayli knew murderers were keen on lulling the police into a false sense of security before striking again.

The ART unit pulled up alongside her and took over the operation. They ordered Melinda to get out of the car and to lie facedown on the ground. One of the team then approached her, pointed a gun at her head as he searched her for a weapon, then placed her in cuffs. When he shouted that it was all-clear, two police officers swooped in and hauled the woman to her feet.

Kayli marched towards her. "You'll regret the day you ran down a police officer, bitch."

Melinda Walton tipped her head back and laughed. "I doubt that!"

"Take her in, and throw her in a cell. I'll deal with her and her accomplice later."

The suspect's brow furrowed. "What accomplice? I didn't have one. I didn't need one."

Kayli's eyes narrowed. "There's no point trying to save your boyfriend now. He's just as guilty as you."

Melinda glared at her. "Call yourself a copper? You haven't got a bloody clue, woman. He's nothing to do with this. All this was about punishing him."

"Punishing him for what?"

"Dumping me. Yeah, we might be together again now, but that only happened since I killed his girlfriend and that kid of theirs."

"You *knew* about the baby?"

"Of course I did. I read her notes at the surgery, knew that I would lose him forever if he found out about the baby."

Kayli shook her head. "You twisted, deranged, selfish individual."

Melinda smiled. "Thanks, I tried my best. Glad I managed to pull it off."

Kayli stepped closer to her. "You'll be laughing on the other side of your face when you're banged up in prison and the inmates learn that you intentionally killed a pregnant woman because a man had the audacity to jilt you."

Her eyes narrowed, and she leaned forward, her nose virtually touching Kayli's. "It was worth it, and I'd do it all over again if I had to."

Kayli stepped back a couple of paces. "Get this bitch out of my sight before I do something I'll later regret."

She watched the officers manhandle Melinda and secure her in the back of a patrol car, then she turned to the ART commanding officer. "Thanks for your help. Let's hope the streets of Bristol will be safe for the foreseeable future."

"Until the next lunatic decides life has treated them unfairly," the inspector replied.

Kayli headed back to the station to share the news with Donna and Graeme in person. She walked up the stairs and into the incident room. Donna was on the phone to someone and had her finger pointing in the air to get Kayli's attention. She crossed the room towards the constable and looked over her shoulder at her notes.

"Thanks, I'll pass that message on to DI Bright." Donna hung up. "That was Forensics, boss. They finally got the machine working and managed to read the serial number on the bike. It's registered to a Douglas Walton."

"Melinda's relative—her father, perhaps?"

"It would appear so. He died at the beginning of last year."

"Okay, that clears one thing up and firms up that we've got the right person banged up in the cell, not that there was any real doubt about that. What I'm confused about is Lincoln James's part in all this."

Donna frowned. "Carmen's boyfriend? I'm not with you, ma'am."

Kayli perched on the desk behind her and filled Donna and Graeme in about what went on during her detour.

"So you recognised her from his bar? That's how you caught her?" Donna nodded her approval. "Great detective work."

"Thanks. I wish I could feel jubilant about it, but with Dave still in hospital, that ain't going to happen. I nipped back and placed Lincoln in a cell with the intention of questioning him later. He protested his innocence all the way out of his bar and during the drive back here. You know what? After listening to Melinda's version of events, I think I've ballsed up."

"Surely not, boss," Graeme piped up.

"Well, they can both sweat it out in the cell overnight. I'm going to nip into the DCI, bring her up-to-date on things, and then shoot back to the hospital. You guys can get off at your usual time. We'll have a celebratory drink when Dave's up and about."

"Agreed," Donna stated with a smile. "Send him our best wishes when he wakes up, boss."

"I'll be sure to do that." Kayli left the incident room and ran along the hallway to DCI Davis's office. "Is she in?" she asked Fiona.

"Just about to go to a meeting in the city. Go through. I'm sure she won't mind if it's a quick one."

"Thanks, it will be." Kayli knocked on the door and pushed it open when DCI Davis summoned her. "Hello, ma'am. Can I have a quick word? I'm aware you're on your way out. I have good and bad news to share."

"Well, don't just stand there. You've certainly got my attention, Inspector. I'll have the bad news first."

"Umm ... Dave Chaplin is in hospital."

"What? How?"

"The suspect we were after mowed him down. He's in surgery, has been for a few hours. They can't give us a proper prognosis until they've opened him up. The doctor is giving him odds of fifty-fifty."

The DCI fell back in her chair as if someone had just jabbed her in the chest with an iron bar. "Shit! That doesn't sound good. Is there anything I can do? Does his partner know?"

"Suranne is at the hospital now. I'm going back there after I leave you, if that's all right?"

"Of course it's all right. Although, I would rather you were out there trying to find the person responsible for this, Inspector."

Kayli smiled. "That's the good news, ma'am. We apprehended her a little while ago, and she's in a cell downstairs."

DCI Davis catapulted upright again and punched the air. "Good job. Does this mean the streets of Bristol will be safe tonight?"

"I bloody well hope so, ma'am."

"Then get out of here. Your partner needs to hear the news first-hand when he wakes up."

Kayli jumped to her feet and saluted DCI Davis. "Yes, boss. See you tomorrow."

"You will, indeed. I want to be involved in the interview with the suspect."

"Ma'am? Don't you trust me?"

"Of course I trust you. No one tries to kill one of my officers and gets away without feeling my wrath, Inspector. The suspect won't know what's hit her when we go in there."

"Yes, ma'am." Kayli rushed out of the office then skipped down the stairs and out to the car.

Within twenty minutes, she was back in the family room at the hospital with Suranne, sharing the good news. Their buoyant mood dissipated when the doctor walked in the room. His face was unreadable. Kayli crossed her fingers and closed her eyes as he delivered the news they'd been waiting for.

"We think we've managed to stem the internal bleeding, as that was our greatest concern. We've strapped up his ribs. They'll mend themselves over the next few weeks, and he'll have his leg in plaster for a few months. He's in recovery. You should be able to go and see him soon."

Kayli and Suranne hugged each other tightly. Tears running down their faces, they pulled apart and thanked the doctor for taking care of Dave so well.

"All in a day's work." He smiled and left the room.

They walked into the recovery room to find Dave still unconscious after his operation. Suranne kissed him on the cheek and stood back to allow Kayli to get near to the bed. She leaned down to whisper in his ear, "We got the bitch, Dave. We'll make her pay for what she did to you."

Suranne tapped her on the shoulder and pointed at his hand. His finger twitched slightly.

Kayli smiled at Suranne. "He understood me. He's going to be all right."

A croaky voice said, "Of course I'm going to be bloody all right. It would take more than just a lunatic woman driver to keep me down." One of his eyes opened, and a smile appeared.

They all laughed. "It's great to have you back, partner."

"Take my word on this, it's great to be back. Why do I feel like a tractor has reversed over me a dozen times?"

"You've got a broken leg and a couple of busted ribs. The doctor says you'll make a full recovery. Look, Dave, if you wanted time off work, you could have done what normal people do, and put in a holiday request. You always have to go one step further, don't you?"

Dave shook his head in despair and winced. "I'll be back to work in a week or so. A broken leg ain't gonna keep me at home. No offence, love." He grinned at Suranne.

"I'm glad to hear it. The last thing I want is you under my feet, feeling sorry for yourself," Suranne replied, playing along with his exceptionally high spirits, given the circumstances.

Kayli left, giving Suranne time to be alone with Dave before exhaustion overcame him. She drove home, feeling excited for a number of reasons, but as soon as she inserted her key in the front door, the loneliness hit her like a sucker punch. She flicked the switch on the kettle then looked in the fridge for something to eat, but it was virtually empty. In the cupboard she found a tin of baked beans, so she made beans on toast and sprinkled cheese on top then settled down to eat it.

She spent the next couple of hours jotting down questions she intended to ask Melinda Walton during the interview the next day. She had certain misgivings about the interview, especially as the DCI wanted in on the act, hence her preparation. *Why does life have to be so damn complicated at times?* She fell into bed at ten thirty, her thoughts with Mark, thousands of miles away.

CHAPTER SEVENTEEN

The following morning, not even the pouring rain could dampen Kayli's spirits as she ran through the main entrance of the station. "Bloody monsoon weather out there, Ray. How were our guests last night?"

"Too right, ma'am. Even the ducks will be sheltering from that. The guests had a mixed night, shall we say. He sat in his cell, not a peep out of him. She, on the other hand, demanded attention every hour on the hour, made a right nuisance of herself, according to the night shift."

Kayli puffed out her cheeks and rolled her eyes. "Let's hope she'll be too tired to cause a stink during the interview. I'm sensing I could be wrong about that, though." She leaned in and whispered, "I've got the DCI joining me on this one."

The desk sergeant grimaced. "Ouch, poor you. I better get my guys doing a little tidying up around here if the DCI is going to be around."

Kayli laughed. "We've all got our crosses to bear. I need to get a gallon of coffee down my neck before I tackle the vixen in there. Has the duty solicitor been informed?" She pointed at the cells on her way through the reception area.

"Yes, they're on their way in, ma'am."

It was ten minutes to nine, and she had no idea what time the DCI would be available to join her. Therefore, she bought a coffee from the machine and went into the office to see what had landed on her desk overnight. DCI Davis walked into her office twenty minutes later. "Let's get this over with, Inspector."

Kayli pushed aside her paperwork, sought out the notes she had made at home, and jumped to her feet. "It shouldn't take long, boss. She's had a restless night, and that could work two ways, either in our favour or against us."

"Let's hope it's the former."

They walked down the stairs and into the reception area in silence.

"Sergeant, we're ready for Walton now," Kayli announced.

"Very well, ma'am. Interview Room One is ready for your use. I'll get a constable to bring the suspect in to you."

DCI Davis didn't say much once they were in the interview room. The suspect arrived, with her appointed solicitor, a female Kayli knew and liked, a Miss Banner. The four women sat around the table. Kayli said the necessary verbiage to the tape then looked down at her notes, suddenly feeling nervous due to the DCI's presence. She hoped Walton didn't pick up on her nerves and make a show of her. She had never conducted an interview with the DCI present. "For the tape, can you confirm your name?"

Walton sneered at her. "No comment."

"Maybe it would be wise to have a word with your client before we start, Miss Banner. Perhaps inform her that we have all the time in the world to question her and that 'no comment' answers are not acceptable in an interview of this nature."

Miss Banner smiled and leaned close to Walton's ear. All the time, Walton's hard, steely gaze never left Kayli's.

"Let's try again. Please confirm your name for the tape."

"Melinda Walton."

Kayli nodded her acceptance. "My first question is why you refused to stop your car at your place of work yesterday? And felt the need to run down one of my colleagues, DS Chaplin."

"He shouldn't have been in my way."

"Why were you leaving? What did you have to hide?" Kayli pressed quickly. That was the way she preferred to interview suspects: fast and furious, without allowing them time to think between their answers.

"Duh! Obvious," she said, an evil smile caressing her lips.

"You knew we were closing in on you for the murders of Carmen Drinkwater, Adam Finley, and Brenda Godfrey. Is that correct?"

Walton shrugged.

"You shrugged. For the tape, was that an admission of your guilt?"

"Whatever."

Kayli raised an eyebrow in the solicitor's direction. Miss Banner leaned over and whispered in her client's ear once more.

"I repeat, was that an admission of your guilt? Did you kill the three victims?"

Walton clenched both her fists. Her eyes widened and were ablaze with hatred. "Yes. Yes, I killed them. They all deserved to die."

"Maybe you can tell us why you killed them?"

Walton took a deep breath and let it out slowly through her lips before she answered, "They deserved to die." She pointed at Kayli. "Don't forget the little brat in that equation too."

The solicitor looked up from the notes she was taking and tilted her head at Kayli, asking for an explanation.

"Carmen Drinkwater was with child when Miss Walton forced her off the road. Was that why you killed her?"

Staring at Kayli, Walton gave her a slow, deliberate nod then raised her head again, a smile tugging her lips apart.

Kayli felt sick to the stomach at the woman's obvious pleasure at killing the little one. "Okay, that takes care of Carmen and the baby. What about Adam Finley? Why did you shoot him?"

"He deserved it."

"May I ask why? Wasn't he Lincoln James's best friend? Lincoln James being the man that you were involved with, despite him living with Carmen Drinkwater."

"Yes. He tried to interfere. Kept badgering me every time Lincoln wasn't around. Called me a whore for spreading my legs for Lincoln. He had no idea how in love we were—are. Lincoln was going to leave Carmen. We'd been discussing it for months."

Kayli's eyes narrowed as her brain notched up a gear. "So, when you saw Carmen at the surgery and looked at her notes, you must have been horrified when you found out she was carrying Lincoln's child. Did he assure you they weren't sleeping together?"

"Yes, I was furious that he'd lied to me. He broke off with me not long after. I presumed that she had told him the news about the baby."

Kayli shook her head. "He never knew about the child. Maybe he just got bored of you."

"Never. He loved me as much as I loved him."

"I doubt that. He wasn't prepared to kill anyone who stood in the way of your relationship, unlike you."

Walton's head dropped onto her chest. At last, Kayli saw some form of remorse .

"So tell me. How did Brenda fit into this?"

Her head rose, and their eyes met once more. "She tried to inter-fere. Caught me looking at Carmen's notes at the surgery and sussed that something was going on between Lincoln and me when she saw my reaction to the news about the pregnancy."

"You killed her? For that?"

She hitched up a shoulder. "People have no right to interfere with my future happiness with the man I love."

"Did he really love you, Melinda? After all, he'd already broken off with you once."

Her glare intensified, and she leaned over the table towards Kayli. "Yes, he loved me. We were going to be together. He prom-ised me."

"And yet he never broke off his relationship with Carmen. Were you aware they were planning a wedding?"

She shook her head. "No. He was building up to telling her it was over. Asked me to give him time to find the right moment. I escalated things by killing her. I wanted him, needed him in my life, and knew that he wouldn't come to me with her around."

Kayli glanced at DCI Davis, shook her head, then turned back to Melinda. "What a twisted mind you have. Are you telling me that Lincoln was in the dark about your warped plans? Or was he aware of the murders you have committed in the name of so-called love?"

"He knows nothing and wouldn't have found out either if ..."

"What? My partner and I hadn't been so good at our jobs?"

"Yes," Walton admitted quietly.

"Maybe you were sloppy. If we hadn't made the connection between you and Lincoln after seeing you talking to him at the bar, perhaps you would have got away with all three murders." Kayli clicked her fingers and slapped the side of her head. "But then, you foolishly dumped the Harley. Although you did your best to disguise the serial number, Forensics were able to decipher it and would have led us to you eventually anyway. Your dad must be so proud looking down on you. Is that when your life imploded? When he died?"

"No. My life hasn't imploded. Once I set out to achieve some-thing, I get it."

"Well, thanks for admitting to your crimes. It has certainly made my job a lot easier. Your admittance has ensured that you will spend the rest of your life in prison."

Kayli ended the interview and stood up. "Are you going to sit in on the next interview, Miss Banner? With Lincoln James?"

The solicitor nodded, and Walton turned sharply to look at Kayli. "He's here?" she asked quietly.

Kayli smiled. "He spent the night in the cell next to yours." She walked towards the door. "Take her back to her cell, Constable." Kayli then trotted down to reception. "Ray, do me a favour and get James out of his cell. I want them to see each other."

The desk sergeant winked at her and unhooked a bunch of keys from the wall behind him. He rushed down the corridor and opened James's cell door. Kayli remained just outside the reception area. At one end, a constable was escorting Walton towards her, while at the other, the desk sergeant was accompanying Lincoln James up the long, narrow corridor.

"Lincoln ... I did it for you, my love!" Walton shouted with tears cascading down her cheeks.

Lincoln James seemed confused. His gaze drifted between Walton and Kayli. When the group met in front of Kayli, Walton tried to grab James, but he turned to avoid her grasp as they passed, appearing to be well out of his depth.

"I guess you got your answer whether Lincoln will wait around for you, Melinda," Kayli said smugly.

Walton screamed all the way to her cell. Kayli caught up with James and took over from the desk sergeant. "I think your constable could do with a hand, Ray."

He nodded and ran the length of the corridor to help the constable secure Walton in her cell.

James looked over his shoulder. "Did she really do it?"

"Yep, all three murders. And you know why, Lincoln?"

"I have no idea."

"All because she loved you."

She escorted him to the table and introduced his solicitor then announced to the tape who was in the room.

Lincoln raised his hand to speak before Kayli had a chance to ask her first question. "Please, you have to believe me. I had nothing to do with this."

"Why get involved with Walton in the first place, Lincoln?"

"I was flattered, I suppose. I had been with Carmen for years, and the thought that women still found me attractive was flattering."

"Ah, a man's ego getting the better of him once again. Are you telling me that you had no inclination of what Melinda was capable of?"

"Nothing at all. Even when she consoled me at the bar after Carmen's death, she showed no hint that the accident was down to her. Had I known, I would have rung you right away." He ran a hand through his hair. "Did she really kill all of them?"

"Yes, Adam and Brenda too."

"Why? Why would she kill my best mate?"

"She said that both people interfered with your relationship. Pointed out how wrong she was to be going after you when you were involved with Carmen."

"That's sick."

"It is indeed. I can't believe that you would be taken in by someone with that kind of mentality. You seem a pretty intelligent man to me."

"She was never like that. Showed none of the traits associated with a psychopath. Do you really think I would have spent time with her if she had?"

"Spent time with her? You mean *slept* with her?"

His chin hit his chest. "All right, slept with her. I will regret my actions forever, Inspector. I can assure you of that."

"I'm not surprised. One thing I'd like to know, if I may? Did Jacky know you were having an affair with Walton?"

He shook his head. "Not with Melinda, but she did guess that I was seeing someone."

"That's why she told me not to trust you."

He glanced up, hurt resonating in his eyes. "I regret my actions. Everything I've done over the last six months ... and now I have nothing. I know you'll think this hypocritical of me, but I truly loved Carmen. I'm devastated I'll never see her again or ever meet the child she was carrying ... *my* child."

"Yep, you're a hypocrite," Kayli agreed. "Okay, I don't believe you were involved in the crimes. All you're guilty of is thinking with your dick. Be careful in the future who you choose to share your life with, Lincoln. You're free to go."

"Oh, I will, believe me. Thank you—not just for letting me go without laying any charges, but also for capturing the person who robbed those closest to me of their lives."

Kayli ended the interview and watched the solicitor and James leave the room. DCI Davis stood up, looked down at Kayli, and began to clap.

"That was brilliant. I wanted to give them both hell, but you did an outstanding job by yourself. You're an amazing police officer, Kayli Bright, just in case I don't tell you often enough."

Kayli felt her cheeks warm. "Thank you, ma'am."

They left the room together and walked up the stairs. "How long do they reckon Dave's injuries will keep him off work?"

"According to him, he'll be back next week, parading around here on crutches. I think he'll revel in trying to get the sympathy vote from his colleagues."

"He's welcome to come back, but on crutches, he'll be as much use as a chocolate fireguard. Leave it with me. I'll see what I can do about getting a replacement."

"A replacement? Will the cuts allow that, ma'am?"

DCI Davis smiled. "I'll do my best to get around that tiny issue for one of my best officers." She walked towards her office. She paused and turned. "By the way, the drinks are on me after work in the pub across the road. Invite the rest of the team."

"Wow! Thank you, ma'am. Very kind of you."

EPILOGUE

Kayli, Donna, and Graeme entered the pub to find DCI Davis awaiting them with a bottle of champagne sitting in a bucket of ice. "She doesn't do things by half, does she?" Kayli said out of the corner of her mouth to Donna.

"Apparently not, boss. It's been years since I had a glass of bubbly. Guess we'll be getting a taxi home this evening."

"I think that's a definite," Graeme said, holding back a little with Donna as they approached the bar.

DCI Davis shook hands with the three of them and handed them each a champagne flute as the barman poured the drinks.

"This is totally unexpected, ma'am, but very much appreciated by us all," Kayli said, accepting her glass.

"You're all worth it, I assure you. I'm sure I can wangle it on expenses one way or another. Congratulations."

They all chinked their glasses together.

"To absent friends," Kayli announced, referring to Dave, although Mark's smiling face entered her mind fleetingly as well.

The next few hours were spent in the company of good friends who took it in turns to reflect over their time in the force with some outrageous anecdotes.

At one point, Kayli nipped to the loo, and when she came out, she almost bumped into Giles. "Hello, you. What are you doing here?"

His gaze bounced around the room as he did his best to avoid meeting her eyes.

"Giles, is anything wrong?" she urged.

"I hate to spoil your celebrations, love, but I need to tell you something."

"Now you're scaring the shit out of me. What's wrong? Is it Annabelle? Is the baby all right?" She glanced over at her team to see everyone looking at them, seeming concerned.

"I think you better sit down, love." Giles tried to steer her to a nearby seat, but she snatched her arm out of his grasp.

"Tell me, Giles," she ordered harshly, her head suddenly clearing.

"It's Mark."

Kayli dropped into the seat behind her. "What about him? My God! He's not dead, is he?" Tears misted her eyes.

Her brother shook his head. "No, he's not dead."

Relief instantly flooded every pore. "Thank fuck for that. What's wrong then?"

"Shit! I hate to tell you this, sis, but he's ... Mark has been kidnapped."

"What?" she screeched, drawing the attention of the other patrons in the bar. "By whom?"

"The Taliban."

"No. No, this can't be happening." Sobs wracked her breaths as her world collapsed around her.

"I'm sorry, sis. They're doing everything they can to get him back."

She saw her brother's lips move, but nothing registered in her brain except the thought of Mark at the hands of the evil Taliban, thousands of miles away from her.

THE END

NOTE TO THE READER

Dear Reader,

Thanks for joining Kayli and her team on this treacherous adventure.

There are many more twisted criminals on Kayli and her team's radar, will you join them on this journey?

In the next book Kayli is challenged, not only in career but in her personal life as well. She has many onerous decisions to make.

I guarantee that *HIDDEN AGENDA* will keep you turning the pages after your bedtime.

Grab your copy today.

http://melcomley.blogspot.co.uk/p/hidden-agenda.html

Thank you for your continued support.
M A Comley

P.S. Reviews are like welcome hugs to authors… won't you hug this author today?

Printed in Great Britain
by Amazon